SHADES *of* GRAY

SHADES of GRAY

Carolyn Reeder

ALADDIN PAPERBACKS

First Aladdin Paperbacks edition May 1999
Text copyright © 1989 by Carolyn Reeder

Aladdin Paperbacks
An imprint of Simon & Schuster
Children's Publishing Division
1230 Avenue of the Americas
New York, NY 10020

Also available in a Simon & Schuster Books for Young Readers edition.
The text for this book was set in 11 point Plantin
Printed and bound in the United States of America

The Library of Congress has cataloged the hardcover editions as follows:
Reeder, Carolyn. Shades of Gray
Carolyn Reeder. — 1st ed.
p.   cm.
Summary: At the end of the Civil War, twelve-year-old Will, having lost
all his immediate family, reluctantly leaves his city home to live in the Virginia
countryside with his aunt and the uncle he considers a "traitor" because he
refused to take part in the war.
ISBN 0-02-775810-9 (hc.)
[1. Orphans—Fiction. 2. Uncles—Fiction. 3. United States—History—Civil War,
1861-1865—Fiction. 4. Conscientious objectors—Fiction. 5. Virginia—Fiction.]
I. Title.
PZ7.R25416Sh   1989   [Fic]—dc20   89-31976
CIP   AC
ISBN 0-689-83866-2

in memory of my father,
Raymond B. Owens

SHADES *of* GRAY

ONE

Will sighed and tipped his hat so the brim shaded his eyes from the late afternoon sun. Now, if only he could block out the monotonous creaking of the buggy wheels.

Doc Martin pointed to a small cluster of buildings on the right and said, "Shouldn't be much farther now. They live just a couple of miles beyond the store and the mill."

Will looked at the motionless waterwheel and frowned. The mill wasn't grinding, so food must be as scarce in the Virginia Piedmont as it was in the Shenandoah Valley. Another reason his aunt's family would probably be as sorry to see him as he would be to see them. He scrunched lower in his seat.

The doctor took a handkerchief from his pocket and mopped his florid face. "I know how you feel about coming here, Will," he said, "but it's what your mother wanted. Her instructions were quite clear—if anything happened to her and your father, you children were to go to her sister."

At the mention of his family, Will felt the familiar burning behind his eyes. He clenched his jaw and waited until he could speak without his voice trembling. Then he said stiffly, "She wrote out those instructions a long time ago. That letter you showed me was dated before the war. She'd never have wanted us—wanted me—to live with traitors."

Doc Martin sighed heavily. "We've been through all this before, Will. You know this is the way it has to be, so you might as well make the best of it."

1

Will gritted his teeth. He hated to be preached at. And there was more to come.

"I don't want to hear any more about traitors, either. Your uncle wasn't a traitor. He didn't help the Yankees, he just didn't fight them. I don't approve of that any more than you do, Will, but the war's over. It's time to forget the bitterness."

Forget? Will swallowed hard. It was fine for Doc Martin to talk. The war hadn't ruined *his* life. *His* father and brother hadn't been killed by the Yankees. *His* little sisters hadn't died in one of the epidemics that had spread from the encampments into the city. And *his* mother hadn't turned her face to the wall and slowly died of her grief.

Will pushed back his hat and glared at Doc Martin. "You don't have as much to feel bitter about as I do," he said.

Doc Martin's gray eyes looked sad behind his spectacles. "You don't think four years of seeing young men die is enough to make a doctor bitter?"

Will's anger drained away. "I—I'm sorry, Doc. I guess I wasn't thinking," he muttered. They rode on in silence, and Will felt an empty sadness. This might be the last time he'd ever see Doc Martin. Why had he spoiled their time together?

Finally he asked, "Shouldn't we be there by now? It seems like we've gone at least two miles since the mill."

"We should be getting there," agreed Doc Martin. Reining in the horse, he brought the buggy to a stop beside a girl who was walking along the edge of the road, gathering something into a basket. "Could you tell me if Jed and Ella Jones live near here, miss?"

The girl looked up, her blue eyes wide. Brushing a loose strand of light brown hair off her face with one hand, she nodded, staring from Doc Martin to Will and then letting her eyes linger on Chauncy, the stout Morgan that pulled the buggy. "It's on the left a little way beyond the creek," she said finally, pointing down the road.

Will glanced down at the girl. She looked about ten, two years younger than he. He caught his breath and took a closer look, thinking how much she resembled his sister Betsy. Their eyes met, and Will looked away, embarrassed that the barefoot country girl with a smudge of dirt on her cheek had caught him staring.

"Thank you, miss," said Doc Martin, clucking to his horse.

At the shallow creek, the horse stopped to drink, and Will looked back. The girl was standing in the road, watching them.

They forded the stream easily and turned in at the grassy lane that left the road by a large chestnut tree. Will looked ahead at the house that would be his new home. It was a small house built of squared logs, with a porch across the front and a stone chimney at one end. Nearby stood a still smaller building—he guessed it was the summer kitchen. There was a hen-house with an empty yard, a small barn that obviously had been unoccupied for some time, and several other small, weathered buildings. Beyond the house he could see a garden patch enclosed by a stone fence, but the fields on both sides of the lane lay fallow. As they neared the house, a woman came out onto the porch.

Will had never met his Aunt Ella, but he knew her at once. Her clothes were worn and faded and her hair was graying, but the way she stood and the proud way she held her head reminded him so much of his mother that his chest ached.

3

Doc Martin stopped the buggy, lowered his bulky frame to the ground, and tied the reins to the pasture fence. Will scrambled down and stood uncertainly for a moment, then followed Doc toward the house.

Doc Martin stopped at the foot of the porch steps and doffed his hat. "Mrs. Jones?" he said. "I'm Dr. George Martin. I tended your sister in her last illness and I've brought you her boy, Will."

Aunt Ella drew a quick breath and then hurried down the steps to welcome Will. Suddenly he was confused. Part of him wanted to run to her and be held close, but part of him wanted to back away. Taking a deep breath, he stepped forward and grasped her outstretched hands in his. "Hello, Aunt Ella," he said, trying to keep his voice steady.

Tears welled up in her eyes as she squeezed his hands and said, "I never even knew she was ill. . . . But what about Betsy and Eleanor? Didn't they come, too?"

"I'll unhitch Chauncy and put him in the pasture," Will said, pulling away and leaving Doc Martin to explain how the little girls had died of typhoid last summer. And to tell what had happened to Charlie. The pulse began to pound in his temples the way it always did when Will thought of his brother's senseless death at the hands of the Yankees.

Methodically, Will led Chauncy into the pasture. He knew it was foolish to unhitch the horse when Doc Martin would be leaving soon, but he'd needed to escape. He was replacing the rails in the pasture gate when a voice at his elbow said, "I'll get him a bucket of water."

He turned and saw the girl they'd met on the road, with her basketful of some kind of wild greens. In a flash he realized

4

why she had reminded him of his sister Betsy—she was his cousin Meg!

"He had a drink at the creek," Will said.

"He might want more," the girl said, eyeing the horse wistfully. "The army got our Nell," she added.

Will looked up in surprise. "Did the Yankees come through here?" he asked.

"The Yankees came through, all right. But it was the rebels that got Nell. They took everybody's horses for the cavalry."

Farm horses like Nell probably ended up pulling artillery guns, Will thought as he watched the girl hurry to the barn and come back carrying a wooden bucket. He waited for her to notice that it was full of spiderwebs and shriek and drop it, but she simply wiped it out with a handful of tall grass and headed off toward the spring.

On the porch, Doc Martin and Aunt Ella were still deep in conversation. Will guessed they must be talking about his mother's long illness. He leaned against the fence and watched Chauncy flicking the flies with his tail as he grazed. Will scowled, wishing his cousin hadn't called the Confederates "rebels." How that word grated on his ears! Then he heard soft footsteps behind him and turned to see Meg struggling with the heavy water bucket.

"Here, I'll carry that," he said, hurrying toward her.

"No, I'll take it to him."

Will shrugged and watched her gently pat the horse's flank.

"I really miss our Nell," she said.

"At least the Yankees didn't get her, Meg."

The girl's eyes narrowed and she asked, "How did you know my name?"

He looked away. "I figured it out," he said stiffly. "I'm your cousin Will, from Winchester."

"When I saw you and your pa on the road I wondered who you were!"

"That's not my father," Will said flatly. "My father was killed in the war."

Meg's hands flew to her face. "Oh, I'm sorry!" she said. And then, curiosity getting the better of her, she asked, "But then who is that man you're with?"

"That's Doc Martin. He brought me here." Will kicked at a rock buried in the grass.

Meg stared at him for a moment. "Then your ma must be dead, too," she said slowly, "and he's brought you here to stay."

Still kicking at the rock, Will nodded.

"But what about your sisters? Are they—"

Quickly, he nodded again. "And so's Charlie, my brother. Killed by the Yankees two years ago."

"So you're all that's left of your family."

Will turned away. "Doc's about ready to leave," he said, reaching for Chauncy's halter. He led the horse out of the pasture and hitched him to the buggy. Just as he finished unloading his belongings, Doc Martin came and stood beside him.

"I wish things could be different," Doc said, resting his hand on Will's shoulder. "There's nothing I'd like better than to have you with me in Winchester. But even if your mother hadn't left that letter, it wouldn't have worked out. A bachelor doctor who's out on calls at all hours and away half the night on confinements can't provide the kind of home a boy needs."

Will gave a jerky nod. "I understand, sir."

"These are good people, Will," Doc Martin went on. "Poor, but good. And they're kin. You'll do fine here—it's a lot different from what you're used to, but you'll do fine."

"I know I will, sir," Will said, hoping he sounded more confident than he felt.

Doc Martin climbed awkwardly into the buggy and then looked down at the thin, dark-haired boy. "Good-bye, Will," he said. His left eye began to twitch, just as it had the night he'd come into Will's room to tell him of his mother's death, and without waiting for a reply he urged Chauncy forward.

As the buggy began to roll down the lane, a feeling of desolation almost overcame Will. Aunt Ella laid her hand on his arm, and her touch calmed him a little.

"Let's move your things inside," she said, turning him away from the sight of the disappearing buggy. "You'll have the room where Sam and Enos used to sleep," she continued. "The twins have gone to Ohio to find work—they'll be sending us their pay to help out."

Will barely listened. He was concentrating on regaining his self-control. But when his aunt stooped to lift a small box tied with ribbon, he mumbled, "That's for you. It's some of Mama's things."

Then he picked up the two carpetbags that contained his clothes, his collection of brass uniform buttons, what little was left of last year's school supplies, some photographs taken before the war, and the family Bible—the Bible with his parents' marriage date and all the children's birth dates entered in his mother's beautiful script. And all the dates of death, too. He himself had carefully printed in the date of his mother's death just a week ago.

"What's in here?" asked Meg as she reached for a long package wrapped in brown paper.

"That's my father's saber," Will answered, a note of pride creeping into his voice. "One of his friends brought it when he came to tell us that Papa'd been killed."

Aunt Ella led the way up the porch steps and into the house. After the bright afternoon sun, Will's eyes were slow to adjust to the dark interior, but he could see the big fireplace on one wall, the rocking chairs and trunklike chest arranged around it, and the large oak dining table near the front window. Through an open door on the other side of the room he saw a quilt-covered bed. He shut out the rising memories of the Winchester house and its large, bright, carpeted rooms filled with upholstered furniture. All that would be sold to pay Mama's debts. This was his home now.

Aunt Ella set her box on the table. Then she crossed the room, opened a narrow door, and started up the steep stairs to the attic. The low-ceilinged space had been partitioned into two sleeping rooms. She opened the door on the left and motioned Will to follow her inside.

In the dim light from the window at the gable end of the room, he saw the neatly made bed with its sunburst patterned quilt, a chest, one chair, and a small table. A kerosene lantern stood on the table.

When Aunt Ella saw his glance come to rest on the table, she explained, "Before the war, Sam did his studying there."

"I'll do my studying there, too," Will said, setting down

his carpetbags and taking the package from Meg.

Aunt Ella sighed. "There's been no school around here since the schoolmaster volunteered early in the war. The building's been boarded up ever since—you probably saw it there by the store when you drove in—and with times so hard I doubt there'll be money to hire a teacher this year."

No school in the fall? Will could hardly imagine not having school! After the academy he'd attended had closed because of the war, he'd gone to the classes one of the pastors had held in his home.

The sound of a door opening broke the silence. "It's Pa!" cried Meg, running down the narrow stairway.

Aunt Ella rested her hand on Will's arm. "Come meet your Uncle Jed."

His mouth went dry. In the flurry of meeting his cousin and aunt, he'd momentarily forgotten his dread of living in the same house with a traitor—or with a coward, rather, since his uncle hadn't actually helped the enemy.

What would a coward look like? Will wondered as he followed his aunt downstairs. Expecting to see a frail, stoop-shouldered excuse for a man, he was surprised to find a sturdy man with a broad chest and muscular arms listening to Meg's excited chatter.

"So this is our city cousin," the man said, striding across the room. His high forehead and the dark, appraising eyes below his bushy brows were the only part of his face not covered by a luxuriant brown beard.

Will stared at his uncle's outstretched hand. He couldn't shake hands with a man who had refused to fight for the Southern cause! But he couldn't offend the head of the family that was taking him in, either. Slowly, he raised his right hand and felt it engulfed in the man's strong grasp.

Then his uncle said, "There's two squirrels for you out in the kitchen, Ella."

"I'll make a stew to go with the poke greens Meg cut along the road this afternoon," Aunt Ella said, turning toward the door. "You can bring me some wood for the fire, Will."

Glad to leave the house and his uncle, Will started for the woodshed. He gathered up an armload of split logs, choosing oak and locust to make the fire last.

His aunt smiled her thanks as he stacked the wood beside the stone fireplace that covered the north wall of the summer kitchen. "Now you can get me a potato from the cellar," she said, fanning the small flame she had coaxed from the embers.

Lifting the trap door in the far corner, Will could barely make out a ladder that led into the pitch blackness below.

"The lantern's on the shelf behind you," Aunt Ella said.

He raised the glass chimney, and his aunt touched the wick with a burning broom straw she'd lit at the fire. Then, carefully holding the lantern, he felt his way down the ladder. Will breathed in the earthy smell and savored the sudden coolness as his eyes passed over the shelves of empty canning jars and came to rest on the vegetable bins. He chose the largest of the wrinkled potatoes that covered the bottom of one bin and took it to his aunt.

"I'll split you some kindling now," Will said.

He found a hatchet, chose a piece of pine wood, and seated himself on a stump outside the woodshed. As he began to splinter off strips of wood, Meg joined him.

"Didn't you have slaves to do that sort of work?" she asked.

Will couldn't tell whether she was being sarcastic or not, but he decided to give her the benefit of the doubt. "We had three slaves," he said. "Callie was our cook, and Lizzy looked after the house. Fred did the outside work. He took care of our horses and split the wood and made the garden."

"Did the army get your horses, too?" asked Meg.

"My father was in the cavalry, so he and Fred took the horses."

Meg's eyes widened. "Did Fred go in the cavalry?"

"Fred went with my father, to look after him and the horses."

"But I thought—"

Will interrupted her. "You thought all slaves wanted to run away from their cruel masters, didn't you?" he challenged.

She nodded, her eyes not leaving his face.

"Well, that was true on a lot of big plantations farther south, but some slaves were well treated and cared about their families." Will shaved off more pine splinters. "Our Lizzy looked after Betsy and Eleanor when they were sick. She cried as hard as Mama did when they died."

Tracing a curve in the dust with her bare toe, Meg said simply, "My little sister died, too."

"You mean Beth?" Will said, looking up in surprise.

"She died during the war. After your mother started sending back Ma's letters without even opening them." Meg's voice was cold, and her eyes narrowed.

Will frowned. He hadn't known about that! He got up and went to the woodshed for another log.

"How did Beth die?" he asked when he came back. "Did she catch diphtheria?"

11

Meg shook her head. "Rebel scouts took our cow, and without any milk, she sickened. Wasted away, Ma said." She sighed. "I still miss her sometimes." Then, as an afterthought, she added, "Bessie was such a good milk cow, it seemed a shame to turn her to beef."

Will felt a wave of anger surge through him. "You should think of Nell and Bessie as your family's contribution to the war, since your father wouldn't fight," he said in a voice that was deadly quiet.

Meg's hands tightened into fists. "Pa saw no need to go to war so that rich people could keep their slaves!" she said.

Will dropped the hatchet and stood up to face his adversary. "Don't you know anything? The war wasn't about slavery—it was about states' rights! People in the South were tired of being told what to do by a government hundreds of miles away in Washington. They wanted to live under laws made by their own state governments instead. The war was about states' rights, Meg."

"They just said that so men who didn't own slaves would fight in it!" Meg shot back. "Anyway, people's rights are more important than states' rights, and Pa had the right to decide not to fight in the war!"

Will looked scornfully at his cousin. "If men had the right to decide whether or not to fight when their country's at war, there wouldn't be any armies," he said.

Meg met his gaze. "I know of two armies we'd both have been a lot better off without," she said. Then she turned and walked back to the house, her head held high.

Will muttered an oath he'd learned from a young officer who had been quartered in their house one of the times Winchester was in Confederate hands. Then he scooped up an armload of kindling and headed for the summer kitchen.

Will was glad when the evening meal was over, even though he was still hungry. He knew he was stretching the family's meager food supply, and he was ill at ease in spite of his aunt's attempts to make him feel welcome.

He excused himself and climbed the stairs to his attic room. First he put his clothes in the chest and arranged the family Bible, his copybook with its few precious blank sheets, and his pen and ink bottle on the table under the window. Trying not to think about an autumn without school, he slipped his slate into the chest and tucked it under his' clothes.

Will hesitated a moment, holding his small package of family photographs. Then, resolutely, he put them with his slate at the bottom of the chest. That done, he found a nail in the wall where he could hang his father's saber and the pouch of uniform buttons he'd collected from the battlefields and army camps near town. Then he threw himself across the bed.

He felt at ease with Aunt Ella and he guessed he'd learn to get along with Meg. Already they seemed almost like family, probably because they reminded him of Mama and Betsy. But he knew he'd never feel comfortable around his uncle. Imagine the son of a Confederate cavalry officer having to accept charity from such a man! He'd be courteous, and he'd help out all he could to make up for being an extra mouth to feed. But he'd never call him Uncle Jed. Never!

With that decided, Will flopped over on his stomach and fell into an exhausted sleep.

TWO

Will woke early and slipped downstairs and out onto the porch. Uncle Jed was coming back from the spring with two buckets of water. He set one inside the door of the summer kitchen and carried the other to the porch, where he filled a dishpan and began to wash his face. Will thought wistfully of the pitcher of hot water Lizzy had brought to his room each morning and poured into the porcelain bowl that stood on the small marble-topped table. He gave a start when his uncle turned to him and spoke.

"Not much reason to get up this early nowadays, with no stock to feed and water. But old habits die hard." He dried his hands and went on. "I didn't take sides in that there rebellion, but I'll be doggoned if both sides didn't take me! It'll be a long time before this place recovers from the war."

"It'll be a long time before *Virginia* recovers!" Will said.

The man nodded. "You've seen more of that than I have," he agreed, "coming through the Valley like you did on your way here."

It was Will's turn to nod as he thought of the spoiled fields and the blackened squares of earth where barns once stood, and of the occasional skeletal chimney rising from the charred ruins of a home.

"I saw you chopped some kindling for your aunt. Why don't you go on over and make the fire so she can start breakfast?"

Will headed for the kitchen, glad for an excuse to end the conversation.

———————

Breakfast that morning was a thin gruel that didn't taste like anything Will had ever eaten.

"It's made from the buckwheat the Yankees didn't get," Meg said. "Their foragers never found where Ma hid it." She grinned at Will from across the table. "Ma put pillow slips on six sacks of grain and set them right on top of the feather pillows on the beds. When she tucked the quilts in, you couldn't tell they were there!"

"Six sacks wasn't much, but it's given us enough meal for gruel most mornings and pancakes now and then," said Aunt Ella. "Meg grinds the grain in the coffee mill."

Will spooned up the rest of the gruel. It was better than nothing, but he was still hungry. He wondered what they would have had for breakfast if his aunt hadn't been so clever.

Uncle Jed pushed himself away from the table. "I've set up a new trap line, Will, and I'm going out to check it now. I want you to come along so you can learn the way and take it over."

Will got up and followed his uncle out the door, hoping that he'd be a quick learner.

Uncle Jed set a fast pace as they crossed the empty pasture to where the woods began. Ropes of honeysuckle wound their way up the straight trunks of the locust trees at the edge of the clearing, and wild grapevines as thick as Will's wrist hung from the chestnut trees beyond them.

15

The faint path they were following began to rise steeply, but Uncle Jed kept the same fast pace. Will was breathing hard, but he was determined to keep up. He'd show his uncle! He'd show him a town boy could get along in the country! Will felt a sense of relief when they reached the top of a narrow ridge, but his spirits fell when Uncle Jed immediately plunged downhill into a grassy hollow.

Finally they neared a small stream that tumbled over the rocks. "This here's the first trap," said his uncle, barely pausing as he pointed to the small, rectangular box with the door at one end still held open.

"Wait," Will gasped. "I—I need a drink." Dropping to the ground, he lay on his stomach beside the stream and drank the icy water from his cupped hands. He was thirsty, but even more than the water, he needed an excuse to stop for a moment to slow his racing heart. But before he had satisfied his thirst, a rough hand on his shoulder hauled him to his feet.

"What are you trying to do, make yourself sick? Don't you know better than to drink so much at once when you're hot?"

Will jerked away from his uncle and glared up at him. The man's answering gaze was scornful, and Will was the first to look away.

"Don't pull a fool trick like that again," his uncle said, turning to walk upstream.

Will followed a short distance behind, nursing his anger. He knew not to drink too much! He watched his uncle stop at intervals to check the other traps. By the time they reached the last empty trap, Will's legs ached, and he was so drenched with sweat that his shirt stuck to his back.

Uncle Jed shook his head. "It's a bad time of year for trapping," he said. "Rabbits don't show much interest in the bait now that there's so much else to eat. Fall and winter's the time to trap, and the pelts are worth more then, too. But when your family's hungry. . . . " His voice trailed off. Then he turned to Will and said brusquely, "Well, now, let's see if you can find your way back."

Will set off, intent on proving that he could meet any challenge his uncle set for him. It would be easy enough to follow the creek downstream, but how would he know where to start back up to the ridge? And then it dawned on him—he had counted a dozen traps on the way upstream, so he'd know to climb to the ridge when he found the twelfth trap.

He had counted ten of them when Uncle Jed called after him, "Hey! You've missed your turn!"

Will's face reddened. How could he have overlooked not one, but two of the traps? Wearily, he trudged back to where Uncle Jed stood under a dead cherry tree. He made a mental note to look for its smooth gray trunk and the chunks of bark that lay on the ground below it so he wouldn't make the same mistake the next time. And then he groaned inwardly at the thought of dragging his aching body along this route again. And again. And again. . . .

The faint path twisted and turned as it descended steeply from the ridge. Several times Will almost lost it; but when he stopped and scanned the forest floor ahead of him, he was always able to see where their feet had scuffed up the matted leaves. How relieved he was when he could see a clearing ahead and knew they were almost back to the pasture fence! He'd done it! He'd shown his uncle! But he didn't have long to savor his success.

17

"You'll lead the way tomorrow," Uncle Jed said as they stepped into the sunlight.

Will gulped. "I—I don't think I'm ready for that yet, sir."

"I'll show you again, then. And call me 'Uncle Jed.' I don't like to be called 'sir.' "

Will didn't answer. He'd try to remember not to say "sir," but he wouldn't call him "Uncle Jed." He'd already decided that. A man who'd refused to fight for the South was no family of his.

"Go tell your aunt she'll not be cooking any rabbits for dinner," his uncle said when they came into the barnyard. "Then you can help Meg hoe the garden. I've got some repairs to do on the barn, 'cause someday I aim to have critters living there again."

Will started for the house. Inside he found Aunt Ella sitting at the big oak table with Mama's things spread out around her. A lump rose in Will's throat when his eyes fell on the little ivory-backed mirror he'd seen his mother use so often, the tortoise shell combs she'd tucked into her thick, dark hair, and the roll of Belgian lace she'd been saving to decorate a new dress after the war was over.

Aunt Ella looked up at him. "I missed her letters so those last years!" she said, her eyes moist. "But I understood," she hastened to add. "I knew she couldn't disobey her husband when he forbade her to write on account of Jed not being in the war. I would have written to her, anyway, but. . . . " Her voice trailed away as she absently wound the lace around her fingers.

Disobey her husband? Papa had been white with anger when he learned that Uncle Jed refused to fight for the South, but

Will hadn't known that he'd put a stop to the letter writing. And Aunt Ella made it sound like Mama would have continued their correspondence. Why, then it was Papa who had sent Aunt Ella's letters back unopened!

Will was confused. Was it possible Mama hadn't cared that her sister's husband refused to fight for the Confederacy? That she really had meant for him to come here in spite of that? But if that was so, why hadn't she written to Aunt Ella after Papa was killed? Had she thought that would be disloyal to his memory?

Aunt Ella reached for the little silver frame that held the tintype of Will's grandparents. "When our parents died," she began, interrupting his thoughts, "all of us children were parceled out to various neighbors and relatives."

Will shifted his weight from one foot to another and cleared his throat. He had often heard the story of how his mother was adopted by a rich spinster cousin in Winchester, while his aunt had been taken in by a family in Culpeper County.

"We hadn't seen each other since your mother's wedding, but all those years we wrote every other week until—" Aunt Ella paused, then hurried on. "And ever since the war ended this spring I'd been hoping I'd hear from her." Her voice broke, and she covered her face with her hands.

Will took a tentative step toward his aunt but then turned and hurried out the door. He was halfway to the barn when he realized he hadn't delivered his uncle's message. Slowly he walked back to the house. Aunt Ella was retying the ribbon around the box that held Mama's things.

"I was supposed to tell you there weren't any rabbits on the trap line," he said from the doorway.

19

Aunt Ella looked up. "I'll make do," she said, smiling.

"Maybe I just imagined she was crying," Will muttered as he retraced his steps toward the barn. But he knew he really hadn't. He stopped for a moment in the shade of the oak that towered over the barn and watched his uncle riving shingles. Uncle Jed had clamped one end of the shingle he was working on to an upright section of log and pressed the other end against his stomach. As he pulled the sharp blade of the two-handled draw knife toward him, shaving curls of wood off the side of the shingle, Will watched in fascination, half hoping the blade would slip.

When Uncle Jed glanced up, Will reddened guiltily and stepped inside the toolshed to look for a hoe. Since he had often watched Fred tend their small garden while he listened to the tales and fables the old slave loved to tell, he didn't think he'd have any trouble working around the roots of the plants and chopping out the weeds.

Meg waved to him from the center of the garden. "Come work over here, so we can talk," she called.

Will glanced at the long, evenly spaced rows of vegetables. In a few more weeks they'd have enough to eat, he thought with satisfaction as he began to hoe a row of beans.

"Not like that!" Meg cried. "Here, let me show you."

Will was embarrassed. What must his cousin think of him? "Fred always did the gardening at home," he muttered as he began hoeing again.

"I can't imagine having somebody else do your work for you," Meg said. "Didn't you feel kind of useless? Hey, don't hoe so near those bean plants! We don't have very many as it is!"

20

"Why didn't you plant more?" Will asked, wishing his cousin wouldn't watch him so closely. He hoped he didn't look as awkward as he felt.

Meg answered, "We ate so many dried beans over the winter there were only a few left for seed." She made a face. "Those beans kept us from going hungry, but without salt pork to cook with them, they sure weren't very tasty."

Will knew what she meant. His family, like most of their neighbors, had practically lived on dried beans during the past two winters, and they hadn't had salt pork, either. "How come your pa doesn't raise hogs?" he asked.

Meg looked up. "He used to raise two every year. He'd work a couple weeks at harvest time for ol' man Smythe, and in the spring he'd get two piglets in return. Pa'd notch their ears and let them forage in the woods till winter, then he'd herd them back and feed them corn for a couple of weeks before he butchered them."

"So did the army get your pork last year?"

Meg shook her head and grinned. "No, an old bear got it. You see," she went on as she skillfully drew the dirt high around a potato plant with the side of her hoe, "Pa heard that the rebel scouts were coming 'round again, so he and the boys loaded everything out of the meat house onto his slide and dragged it way back in the woods. They hung it high up in a tree. Then they came home and took the top hinge off the meat house door so the door would just hang there, and they tossed some dirt and dead leaves inside and swept them around so it would look like the place hadn't been used for a long time.

"When the scouts got here, they didn't even go inside—

21

just looked in and went on their way. But when Pa and the boys went to get the meat, all they found was some scraps and gnawed-on ham bones. And big ol' bear tracks all around and scratch marks on the tree from its claws."

Will hoed in silence, torn between a grudging respect for his uncle's cleverness and disgust because meat that could have fed the South's hungry soldiers had been eaten by a bear.

"Did your pa get any piglets this year?" he asked at last.

Meg's face fell. "Ol' man Smythe didn't ask Pa to help last fall."

Will didn't answer. Another winter with no pork, he thought glumly as he loosened the soil around the roots of the next plant. He had done just over half of his second row, but already his shoulders were beginning to ache, and sweat was running down his face and stinging his eyes. He looked up as Aunt Ella came into the garden carrying a split-oak basket.

"I'm going to thin these turnips for our dinner," she said. "They'll be a nice change from the wild greens we've been having. And I'll stew up the last of the dried apples."

Will was relieved that the tiny turnips and their greens wouldn't be the entire noon meal. But how he wished it were dinnertime now! Already the handle of the hoe was raising blisters on his hand, and the combination of hunger and the hot sun was making him feel light-headed.

"Will," his aunt said, straightening up and looking at him, "I need you to carry a bucket of water to the kitchen and then to chop me some kindling."

What welcome words! He leaned his hoe against the stone fence and set off. At the spring, he poured a bucket of water over his head, bracing himself for the icy shock. Then he refilled the bucket and carried it to the kitchen, where the fire was burning down to glowing coals. As he moved away, he saw the nearly full basket of kindling he'd cut the afternoon before and wondered why his aunt had asked for more. A wave of shame swept over him. Aunt Ella had guessed how tired and sore he was and had given him a chance to work sitting down in the shade! And he was going to do it—while his cousin worked in the hot sun. Her words came back to him: "I can't imagine having somebody else do your work for you."

Miserable, he went to the woodshed, picked up the hatchet, and chose a pine log. When he came outside, Aunt Ella was carrying her basket of turnips and greens into the kitchen. He heard the sound of hammering and looked up to see his uncle nailing the newly rived shingles onto the barn roof. How hard they all worked! And how little they had to show for it.

Will thought of Doc Martin's parting words: "You'll do fine here—it's a lot different from what you're used to, but you'll do fine." He carefully placed the hatchet blade in a crack near the center of the log and whispered, "I *will* do fine here. I will! And I'll show them I'm not useless, too."

THREE

After their noonday dinner, Aunt Ella said, "Meg, take Will down to the river where Sam and Enos used to fish. Maybe he can catch something for our supper tonight."

Will was elated. "I'll go dig some worms for bait!"

"The twins always used grasshoppers," said Meg. "I'll help you get some out in the pasture."

They walked slowly through the tall grass, swooping down

23

on the greenish-brown insects with their cupped hands. As Meg shook a grasshopper into the canning jar Aunt Ella had given them, Will thought of how his sisters had squealed when they saw even the smallest insect. But Meg didn't flinch at touching the raspy legged creatures.

"We've got more than a dozen now," she said, holding the jar up for a better look. "Here, tie your handkerchief over the top while I find Sam's fishing pole."

"How far is it to the river?" Will asked as they set off.

"It's through the woods a ways. We could go to the millpond instead, if you want."

Thinking of his experience in the woods that morning, Will said, "That sounds like a good idea. And I know the way there—I saw the mill when we came yesterday."

"Well, I'm going with you, anyhow," said Meg, her chin set in determination. "I'd rather sit in the shade than hoe, same as you would."

Will's face burned. Why hadn't he gone back to the garden after he'd carried Aunt Ella's water to the summer kitchen?

They walked along without speaking for a few minutes. Will deliberately set a fast pace, but Meg seemed to have no difficulty keeping up. Finally she broke the awkward silence.

"Mmm, do you smell that?"

Will nodded, aware now of a delicate, roselike fragrance.

"We'll have more blackberries than we can pick in a few weeks," his cousin went on, gesturing toward the blossom-covered bramble bushes growing along the roadside. "When we had Bessie, we'd eat big bowls of blackberries and cream with every meal."

"We picked berries at home, too," Will said, "and Callie'd

24

make blackberry pies and blackberry cobbler. And she'd make jam. 'Course, that was before the war, when we still had sugar."

"Whatever became of Callie and Lizzy and Fred?" Meg asked.

"After Papa was killed, Fred came back and worked for us till the war was over. Now he works at the livery stable in town. Callie got a job as cook at the hotel, but Lizzy stayed to take care of Mama. Doc Martin said he'd try to find a place for her." He kicked away a stick that lay in the road. "I guess I'll never see any of them again."

"I hadn't thought you might be missing your slaves, too," Meg said in surprise. "I miss Sam and Enos, but that's different because they're my brothers."

"I wonder what it's like in Ohio?" Will asked, quickly changing the subject.

"Well, they have cream for their blackberries in Ohio, 'cause the rebel army never camped nearby and took all the cows for beef. They've got plenty to eat, 'cause the rebel scouts never came through and took their harvest and their salt pork. And they could plant all their fields this spring, 'cause they still had horses to pull their plows and they hadn't eaten most of their seed potatoes and beans to get through the winter."

Will struggled to control his anger. "They'll have flour to make crusts for blackberry pies, 'cause the Yankee cavalry didn't ride through their fields all strung out in a row and mash the wheat down into the ground. And they can grind their wheat, 'cause Sheridan's army didn't burn their mills. And," he went on, his voice rising, "they'll have apples and

25

cider next winter, 'cause the Yankees didn't chop down their orchards for firewood. And in Ohio—"

"Stop! Stop it!" cried Meg, clapping her hands over her ears. "I don't want to hear any more about the war!"

Will stopped and stared at her. She stood in the middle of the road, dust-covered feet showing beneath a faded skirt and the basket that hung on her raised arm sticking out at an odd angle. Her blue eyes were dark with anger.

"Well, you started it," he muttered, looking away.

"You were the one who asked what it was like in Ohio," Meg reminded him. They walked for a while in stony silence. Then Meg said, "I wouldn't want to go to Ohio, anyway. Virginia's our home, and Pa says now that the war's over it'll be a good place to live again."

"I guess when he can replace the livestock and plant all his fields again, your life won't be much different than it was before the war," Will said. Then, remembering Beth, he added, "Your little sister could have died even if the army hadn't got your cow."

"Your sisters could have died of typhoid in peacetime, too, you know."

Will looked away. "The epidemic started in the army camp," he said stiffly. "They wouldn't have died if it hadn't been for the war. And neither would Papa and Charlie and Mama. I'd still be living with my family in Winchester if it hadn't been for the war—if it hadn't been for the Yankees."

"Your pa chose to fight in the war," said Meg, "so you—"

"Papa had no choice! He was a man of honor, and when his country needed him, he had no choice but to go to war!"

26

"My pa's a man of honor, too, and he says a person always has a choice!" Meg said firmly. "He says you have to look at a situation and measure the good against the bad and then do what you think is right, no matter what other people do. And he didn't think it was right for him to go and kill other men over something that didn't matter one way or the other to him." Then she added quickly, "Now I'm not saying your pa was wrong to fight in the war, 'cause I know it made a difference to him how things turned out. All I'm saying is—"

"Of course it wasn't wrong! He was fighting for a cause he believed in! Can't you understand that?"

"I can understand that, all right. The question is, why can't you understand that my pa *didn't* fight for a cause he *didn't* believe in?"

Will didn't know how to answer that. They walked on in silence again, the buzzing of the insects on the blackberry blossoms and the soft scuffing of their bare feet on the dusty road the only sounds. But Meg couldn't be quiet for long.

"There's something I can't figure out," she said. "Your brother Charlie was the same age as Sam and Enos, and you said he was killed two years ago. That would have made him only fourteen. How could he be in the army so young? Was he a drummer boy?"

The question came almost as a physical shock to Will. Surely Doc Martin had told Aunt Ella what had happened. Hadn't she told Meg? "I never said he was in the army," he said, walking faster.

Meg's mouth fell open. "But—but you told me he was— was killed by the Yankees!"

"He was shot by a Yankee sentry," Will said reluctantly.

27

Meg's jaw dropped again. "They shot a plain, ordinary boy? Why did they do that?"

Will turned to her, his dark eyes blazing. "I don't want to talk about it!" he shouted. "I just don't want to talk about it!"

Meg fell back, and he walked on ahead, trying to ignore the throbbing in his temples. He picked up a stone and chucked it into a puddle in the road. Why did Meg have to ask? Wouldn't he ever be allowed to forget the horror of his brother's death?

By the time he saw a roadside spring ahead, Will had regained control, and when Meg caught up, he offered her the filled dipper. "Want some?" he asked.

She nodded. "The mill's just around the curve," she said, replacing the dipper.

Will drew a deep breath, relieved that Meg wasn't the kind of person who sulked and held things against you. As they drew near the mill, he saw three older boys fishing in the pond near the motionless wheel.

"Let's sit under that tree," said Meg, pointing to a large sycamore on the far side of the pond.

Will baited his hook and tossed in his line. The grasshopper floated on the surface for a minute or two, moving just enough to make a circle of ripples on the still water. Then it slowly began to sink. Will was just about to sit down on the bank when he saw the boys who had been fishing near the mill wheel making their way around the pond.

"We should have gone to the river," Meg said.

As the boys drew nearer, Will felt apprehensive. Their swaggering walk signaled that they weren't coming over just to say hello.

"Who's your feller, Meg?" taunted the tallest of the three, stopping a few feet away.

"Oh, he's not my feller," Meg said, looking innocently at her questioner. "He's my cousin, Will Page. His father was killed in the war and his mother's dead, so he's come to live with us." Then she turned to Will and said formally, "Will, I'd like you to meet Hank, Patrick, and Amos."

Just then Will's cork dipped beneath the surface and he felt a tug on his line. He jerked the pole, swung it to the right, and after a brief struggle landed a good-sized bass. The boys backed up a few steps to keep from being splashed.

Will knelt and grasped the flopping fish, skillfully removed the hook, and threaded a string through its gills. Tying the other end of the string to the branch of a small box alder growing at the water's edge, he tossed the fish back into the pond to keep cool. Then, wiping his hands on his pants legs, he turned to the three boys. Stepping toward them he said, "Pleased to meet you. Which one of you is Hank?"

"I am," said the tall, lanky boy who had spoken earlier. He looked about fourteen. Gesturing reluctantly toward a heavyset boy a little younger, he said, "That's Amos, and this here's Pat." Patrick had red hair and freckles.

Hank turned to Meg again, but before he could speak, Will asked, "How many fish have you all caught today?"

The boys looked at one another. "Oh, we caught some little ones and threw them back," Hank said unconvincingly.

"You know," Amos chimed in, "little ones about this long,"

and he used his hands to show the length of Will's fish.

"Those little ones are the most tasty," Will said, turning around and dropping to one knee to shake another grasshopper out of the jar. The skin on the back of his neck crawled with anxiety. He didn't like to turn his back on the boys.

His worst fears were realized when a menacing voice close behind him said, "How'd you like to go for a little swim?"

Without looking around, Will said, "I'd like that just fine, Hank. Is there a swimming hole around here? We could race."

"Race?" Hank sounded uncertain now. "I don't think our swimming hole's big enough for racing. And it's too far away."

"Come on, Hank. It's getting kind of crowded around here," Patrick said. "Let's go somewhere else."

"Yeah, somewhere that doesn't smell so fishy," said Amos.

Will baited his hook and tossed in his line. He watched the widening circles, waiting until the last one reached the shore and the grasshopper had sunk out of sight before he turned his head. The boys were gone! With a sigh of relief, he sat down on the grassy bank.

"You were wonderful!" cried Meg, plopping down beside him.

Will didn't know what to say, so he brought his index finger to his pursed lips and stared intently at the water. Meg covered her mouth with her hands.

"I'm sorry, Will," she whispered.

They sat in companionable silence, enjoying the occasional breeze that blew across the pond and watching the blue-backed swallows' skittery flight as they skimmed insects off the water's surface. Too soon, it was time to start for home.

" 'Those little ones are the most tasty,' " Meg said as Will retrieved his fish.

He grinned, hoping that his success at the pond would make Meg forget his lack of gardening skill and stamina.

After her enforced silence, Meg chatted gaily as they walked toward home. But as they rounded the curve and saw three familiar figures lounging at the spring, her words died away.

Will's heart began to pound against his ribs. "Don't slow down, Meg," he said. "And don't act like you're afraid."

She nodded and began chatting with great animation. Nearing the spring, she lifted her hand in a casual wave but kept right on talking to Will until Hank got up and sauntered into the road.

"Hand over that fish, Will-yum," he said roughly.

Will could feel the thump-thumping of his heart, but his voice was steady. "This fish?" he said, looking at it in feigned amazement. "You don't want this little fish!"

Hank glared at Amos, and Will said, "Come on, Meg, we don't want this fishy smell to bother our friends any longer." Will led Meg around Hank, and she began to chatter again. Will held his breath, listening for the scuff of running footsteps behind them, but there was nothing. Finally he allowed himself a quick look over his shoulder and saw that the road behind them was empty. He gave a sigh of relief.

Meg grinned at him. "You did it again! You really showed that Hank!"

Will didn't answer. He knew he hadn't seen the last of Hank and his friends.

FOUR

When breakfast was over the next morning, Uncle Jed looked across the table at Will and said, "So, you don't think you can find your way up the mountain to the trap line."

Will clenched his teeth. Was his uncle trying to embarrass him in front of Aunt Ella and Meg? "Not yet," he said. "I still need to follow you one more time." He hoped one more time would be enough.

Uncle Jed gave a brief nod. "Come along, then."

The grasshoppers that jumped out of the pasture grass reminded Will of his experience at the millpond the day before. Because of Charlie, older boys had never dared to bully him at home. Life had been so much easier back in Winchester— before the war.

They crossed the fence and entered the woods. Soon Uncle Jed made a right-angle turn and began to climb. "Veer left by rotting log," Will muttered to himself. "Bear right past tall pine, and go steeply uphill," he whispered at the next turn. Then, "Make a left by stump with Virginia creeper growing on it, and go straight uphill to the ridge." When they started down into the hollow, Will could hear the creek. They were almost at the first trap!

Out of breath again, Will dropped to his knees by the creek, thinking resentfully that he didn't need anybody telling him how much he should drink. He heard his uncle say, as if to himself, "I wonder if the trap two hundred paces upstream is as empty as this one." Will scrambled to his feet and began to count silently: 1, 2, 3 . . . 198, 199, 200! He stopped and looked around but saw nothing. And his uncle was standing some distance ahead of him, a lifeless rabbit dangling from his hand.

After his initial bewilderment, Will continued his count. When he reached 260, there in front of him was the second trap. All he had to do was count 260 of his own steps, and he'd be able to find every one of them.

He called after his uncle. "I think I can find the rest of the traps now!"

There was no response. He tried again. "Wait for me! I'll lead the way!"

His uncle paid no attention. Panting, Will reached the third trap in time to watch his uncle reset it. Another rabbit lay on the ground at his feet.

"Didn't you hear me holler?" asked Will, his chest heaving.

His uncle looked up at him. "Oh, were you hollerin' for me?" he asked. "How was I to know?"

Will just stared at him. Who else would he be hollering for in the middle of the woods? And then he understood. His uncle wanted to be called by name. Well, he wouldn't do it, and he hoped the man knew why he wouldn't! Turning away, he started upstream, counting silently.

The rest of the traps were empty.

As he hoed the endless rows of carrots and turnips later that morning, Will thought noon would never come. He straightened up to rest his aching back for a moment and flexed his fingers, looking ruefully at the blisters forming on his palms. His stomach rumbled, and he glanced toward the kitchen. A wisp of smoke rose from its stone chimney. Good, he thought. Aunt Ella was starting dinner. Maybe by the time he'd finished another row it would be noon.

But he had done nearly three more rows before he saw Aunt Ella carrying a steaming platter from the summer kitchen. He took his hoe to the toolshed before he went to wash up, his face tingling at the memory of Uncle Jed's words when they'd returned from the trap line that morning: "You'll find your hoe in the toolshed, Will. I put it away for you yesterday." He wouldn't make that mistake again!

Aunt Ella had boiled the rabbits and made a thick gravy for them. Will passed his plate for seconds and didn't complain when Uncle Jed also gave him another helping of tiny beets cooked with their greens. At the end of the meal he sighed with satisfaction. He couldn't remember the last time his stomach had actually felt full.

"I'm going to start repairing the fence around the pasture," Uncle Jed announced. "A lot of the posts are rotting. I'll need your help, Will."

"How long do you think it'll take?"

"Maybe a month, maybe longer."

Will's heart sank. He'd be working side by side with his uncle for at least a month!

In the shed, Uncle Jed gathered up his woodworking tools. Then he turned to Will. "Bring a spade and that mattock," he said, gesturing toward a picklike implement. "You can dig us a pit to char the posts in." When he saw Will's puzzled expression, he explained. "If you char the end that goes in the ground, the wood won't rot so fast."

Will followed him outside, carrying the spade and the heavy

mattock. "Where do you want me to dig the pit?"

"Where do you think it should be?"

Will hesitated a moment and then said, "Near to where we'll be working but away from dry grass that might catch fire."

"That'll be fine," said his uncle.

Frustrated, Will asked, "Well, where are we going to work?"

"Why, right here in the shade of the barn," said Uncle Jed. "I'll bring the post lengths over while you do that."

Still not quite understanding what he was supposed to do, Will chose a spot a little distance away from the barn and the woodshed and began to dig. The pointed end of the heavy mattock bit into the packed earth. By the time his uncle returned, Will's arms and shoulders ached, but he'd dug a good-sized hole.

"Slope the sides some and that'll be fine," Uncle Jed told him. "Then gather up some wood chips and scraps and put them in. You can use the bark that peels off this locust, too. When we get around to charring, we'll be ready."

Will did as he was told. Then he watched while Uncle Jed tapped the sharp-bladed froe with the malletlike wooden maul and split sections off each side of the last few lengths of locust, leaving a center piece with smooth, flat edges.

"I guess you never helped make a fence before—or did much work at all before you came here," Uncle Jed commented.

Will shook his head. At home, there'd been no need for him to work.

"Well, around these parts, a man takes pride in doing things for himself. Now, hand me that auger."

Will had never thought about taking pride in hard, physical work. He handed his uncle the tool and watched him quickly bore two holes in the post about six inches apart, then drop down the distance of two hand spans to make another pair of holes. As he measured out the distance for a third pair he looked up and said, "Remember, now, that's two spans measured by *my* hands."

Thinking of the two hundred paces, Will scowled. He hated to be teased.

"Now bring me that post ax."

Suddenly Will understood what his uncle was doing. He watched him cut away the wood between the two holes he'd bored to make the large vertical opening to slide the fence rails through.

After he had made the first two slots, Uncle Jed handed Will the ax. "Now you try it."

It wasn't as easy as it looked. By the time he was finally through, the third slot had scrapes and scars all around it. Will was embarrassed by his poor effort, but Uncle Jed said, "That's the idea. You go ahead with that while I split out some more posts and bore the holes."

His second attempt showed considerable progress, Will thought. "Where should I put the finished posts?" he asked.

"Wherever you think best."

After a moment's hesitation, Will laid them alongside the pit he'd dug. He turned around and saw Uncle Jed toss aside another post and reach for the next piece of wood. Will picked up a drilled post. If Uncle Jed could split a post and drill six holes in the time it took him to cut out the wood between one pair of holes, by the time he did this post he'd be three behind.

36

He swept his eyes around the pasture fence, trying to estimate how many posts would be needed. He sighed as he picked up the ax. It would take more than a month just to complete this part of the job.

But by suppertime the pile of finished posts gave Will a feeling of satisfaction. At least nobody could say he wasn't earning his keep, he thought as he helped Uncle Jed gather up the tools.

In the morning, Will was the first to leave the breakfast table. "I'm on my way to check the trap line," he announced.

"Are you sure you can find the way?" Meg asked anxiously.

"He can find the way," Uncle Jed said before Will had a chance to answer.

Of course he could find the way! Will thought indignantly as he climbed the fence and entered the woods. Hands in his pockets, he strode along, noticing how very quiet it was. And how different everything looked. Could he have missed his first landmark? He drew a sigh of relief when he spotted the rotting log at the turn.

Will hurried on, watching for the tall pine that was the next landmark. The steep hill seemed endless, and, puzzled, he stopped. He went a few more steps and stopped again, looking carefully all around him. Nothing was familiar. Turning back, he hurried downhill, watching for the pine tree. He must have missed it again! Chest heaving, he started back up the hill, and his eyes came to rest on a boulder—the boulder he had passed just before he'd started to retrace his steps!

Now the silence of the woods seemed ominous. Why were no birds singing? Why was there no breeze? He turned and began to run down the hill. His chest hurt and his breath came in gasping sobs. And then, out of control on the steep slope, he fell. He lay sprawled on the ground for a moment, his head spinning, then slowly sat up. He was bruised, and his elbows were skinned, but that seemed to be the extent of the damage.

"I can't let that happen again," he said aloud. "I can't let myself panic like that."

The sound of his own voice calmed him. He struggled painfully to his feet, and his eyes came to rest on a rotting log. It was the rotting log that marked the first turn! Numbly, he realized that he simply hadn't gone far enough to reach the second landmark. He hadn't missed the pine tree, after all.

Wearily, he started uphill again, passing the place where he had turned back twice. Reaching the pine tree, he continued uphill, turned again at the vine-covered stump, and plodded on.

When at last he came to the creek, Will dropped to his knees and dipped handfuls of the cool water to slake his thirst. After he'd splashed his face and carefully washed the scrapes on his elbows, he started upstream, counting his paces as he made his way from trap to trap. They were all empty.

On the way back, Will tried to make up for some of the time he'd lost, but the sun was high when he climbed over the pasture fence. Nearing the house, he saw Aunt Ella doing the wash in front of the kitchen. Steam rose from the huge iron cauldron where she was stirring the clothes with a wooden paddle, and her hair hung lank. She wiped the perspiration from her face. Will was glad his mama hadn't had to work that hard. At home, Lizzy had always done the wash. And Lizzy would have stayed on with them and worked for wages, now that she was free. And Callie and Fred would have, too, if only—

"I was beginning to worry about you, Will," Aunt Ella said, interrupting his thoughts. "I was afraid you might have gotten lost."

"You don't have to worry, Aunt Ella. I can take care of myself." Just because he'd grown up in town, there was no reason for everybody to think he couldn't learn to get along in the country.

At dinner that noon, Uncle Jed asked Will, "Have any trouble this morning?"

"All the traps were empty," Will answered. Then, because his uncle seemed to be waiting for more, he added grudgingly, "It seemed a lot farther than the other times."

His uncle nodded. "First time Enos walked the old trap line alone, he was so sure he'd missed the first turn, he went back. He was almost home again before he realized he just hadn't gone quite far enough." Then he asked, "How'd you scrape those elbows?"

"Elbows? Oh, I—I fell coming down the hill."

"Going too fast, I reckon," said Uncle Jed.

Will wondered uneasily if his uncle had guessed what had happened.

Working on the fence posts again that afternoon, Will found he was cutting neater slots with the post ax and doing it faster, too. Uncle Jed looked up as Will carried his third completed post toward the growing pile, and Will couldn't resist holding it up to show him.

"That's more like it," Uncle Jed said. "Doesn't look so much like it was gnawed by a varmint."

Will started to work on the next post, furious with himself for seeming to ask for praise. He had to prove that he could do his share of the work—and do it well—even though his family had had slaves to do all the chores. But beyond that, he didn't care what his uncle thought of him.

"We might make a farm boy out of him yet," Uncle Jed muttered as if to himself. And then more loudly, "Get a light from Ella's hearth and start the fire in that pit you dug. When it burns down to coals, we can start charring the posts."

Will scrambled to his feet, pretending he hadn't heard his uncle's compliment. But he was more pleased than he wanted to admit. Why should the opinion of a man he didn't even like make any difference to him? he wondered. In the hot kitchen he plucked a straw from his aunt's broom and stooped to light it in the coals that glowed under the heavy iron pot. As he touched his straw to one of the coals, Will had an idea. Tossing the straw into the fire, he found the ash bucket and shoveled it half full of coals. He carried them to the pit and emptied them in, noticing that his uncle was nowhere to be seen. Then from inside the toolshed he heard the unmistakable sound of a whetstone on a blade and knew Uncle Jed had stopped to sharpen a tool.

Will made another trip for coals, and still his uncle hadn't returned. He started toward the shed to ask how to go about charring the posts but then thought better of it. His uncle would only say, "How do you think you should do it?"

Resolutely, Will began arranging the finished posts so that the bottom ends were in the coals. Not sure what to do next, he gave each one a quarter turn, and then another, and another. Suddenly worried that he might be destroying the results of hours of work, he pulled a post from the coals. The bottom eight inches or so were evenly blackened.

As he lifted the last post from the pit and lay it on the ground, he saw his uncle watching from the toolshed door.

"You sure you never made a fence before?" the man asked.

Will grinned in spite of himself. His uncle was pleased with his work!

FIVE

The next day Will set off for the trap line, confident that this time nothing would go wrong. He reached the first trap with no difficulty, and after a quick drink from the stream, he started off again, hoping that he'd find at least one rabbit to make his walk worth the effort.

As he approached the twelfth trap, he saw that the door had fallen shut. He ran the last few steps and picked up the small wooden box. But what next? He had been too far behind to see how his uncle removed the animals from the traps and how he killed them. He must have wrung their necks, since there hadn't been any blood.

Will had shot squirrels and rabbits, but he'd never killed anything with his bare hands. Gritting his teeth, he pulled the trap door open. The rabbit filled the narrow box, its flanks heaving in terror. Holding his breath, Will reached in, grabbed it, and pulled it out. He felt the animal's muscles tense under the soft fur. And in a flash, the trap was on the ground, the rabbit was gone, and Will's forearm was dripping blood from

41

long rows of deep, curved scratches. He was stunned. How had it all happened so fast?

The cold water of the stream eased the pain in his arm, and the bleeding stopped. Glumly, Will reset the trap, noting that the green apple bait hadn't even been nibbled on. Only the pain in his arm and the emptiness of his stomach kept him from feeling sorry for the terrified animal that had been in the box.

On the way home, Will's arm began to throb. He could imagine what his uncle would say when he found out what had happened: "You're supposed to get the rabbit, not to let him get you!" Or maybe, "If you want something done right, I guess you have to do it yourself."

Why had he been so careless? If it weren't for those claw marks, he could have pretended that all the traps had been empty again. And then he could have asked his uncle casually what he should do when he found a rabbit in one of the traps. Why hadn't he thought to ask him that before he left this morning?

Aunt Ella and Meg were hoeing the garden when Will got back. Taking a deep breath, he called, "I've hurt my arm a little. Can you bandage it for me, Aunt Ella?"

His aunt hurried over. "That needs more than a bandage, young man," she said. "Come on back to the house with me."

After she'd carefully washed her hands, Aunt Ella reached for a can on the mantel. "A little coal oil on that will keep it from getting infected."

Coal oil? Why, that was kerosene! Will braced himself for the searing burn.

"That must smart right bad," Aunt Ella said sympathetically as she tore strips of clean white cloth.

"I'm sorry you got hurt, Will," Meg said, coming in to watch her mother bandage Will's arm.

"I'm just sorry there won't be rabbit stew for dinner," he said through clenched teeth.

"We'll have rabbit stew, anyway," Meg said smugly.

Will looked up, puzzled.

"When I went out to the garden this morning, there was a big ol' rabbit eating the beet tops, so I threw a rock at him. Well, it hit him, and while he was stunned I ran over and killed him with my hoe!" Meg said triumphantly. Then she added, "Ma skinned and cleaned him, 'cause Pa had gone to the store to see if there was a letter from the twins."

Will felt the blood rush to his face. Here he'd walked a couple of miles and come back with nothing to show for it but some gashes on his arm, and she'd gone out to the garden and killed herself a rabbit—accidentally.

"Was there a letter?" he asked at last.

Meg sighed. "Not yet."

At dinnertime Uncle Jed looked at Will's bandaged arm and frowned. "You get kicked by that rabbit this morning?"

Will nodded without raising his eyes.

"I blame myself for that. I should have made sure you knew how to get them out of the trap. Those scratches can really hurt."

Surprised, Will looked up. "You've been scratched?"

"Sure have. When I was about your age, I walked my older

43

brother's trap line for him. Came back all bloody, with no rabbit. At least you didn't lose your rabbit."

Uncle Jed passed Will a plate of stew, and the boy waited for Meg to pipe up with her story. But she didn't say a word.

"Well, I lost my rabbit, too," Will finally admitted. "This is Meg's rabbit." Then he forced himself to say, "Tell your pa how you got it, Meg."

Uncle Jed grinned appreciatively as he listened to Meg tell how she'd killed the rabbit in the garden. "Good for you, Meg! Good for you!" he said when she'd finished. Then he turned to Will. "Well, since we can't count on that happening again any time soon, let me tell you how to get a rabbit out of the trap. You grab the hind legs and jerk him out, and then you whop him on the back of the neck like this," he said, making a chopping motion with the side of his palm.

"Pull him out by the legs and whop him on the back of his neck," Will repeated. But thinking of the warm, furry creature he'd held that morning, he wondered if knowing what to do would make it any easier to kill the next rabbit.

A few days later Will brought back two rabbits from the trap line. After they had been skinned and cleaned, Aunt Ella set one aside and wrapped the other in a cloth.

"Meg, I want you to take this over to Mr. and Mrs. Jenkins. I'll bet they haven't tasted meat since the old man lost his leg in January."

"You're going to send it to *Mr. Jenkins?*" Meg asked in disbelief.

Slipping the neatly wrapped package into an empty flour sack, Aunt Ella handed it to her daughter. "This is as good a way as any to let him know we don't harbor any bitterness," she said.

"Can't Will take it instead?"

Seeing the misery on her daughter's face, Aunt Ella relented. "Very well, but you'll have to show him the way."

Will slung the sack over his shoulder, and the two of them set off. They headed south, past the buckwheat field and then through the orchard and into the second-growth woods beyond.

"Why don't you want to see Mr. Jenkins?" Will asked.

"Well, his two youngest sons were killed in the war," Meg explained, "and last fall when Pa and I were down at the store Mr. Jenkins said he didn't think it was fair for young men to die protecting the rights of people who wouldn't fight for themselves."

Will said nothing. He felt the same way.

Meg went on. "Pa said he agreed with him and asked who he had in mind. Well, Mr. Jenkins said he had in mind a neighbor who always hid in the woods when the conscription teams came through looking for recruits. So Pa said he always made a point of going hunting under those circumstances, but he was sure Mr. Jenkins didn't mean him, 'cause if any of his rights needed protecting he'd protect them himself.

"Well, finally Mr. Jenkins got so angry he challenged Pa to step outside the store and fight him. Pa didn't want to fight an old man, so he said he had no quarrel with him and turned around to leave. And then Mr. Jenkins called him a coward."

Will whistled through his teeth. "What happened then?"

"Pa turned around and walked right up to Mr. Jenkins and took hold of the front of his shirt and yanked him up so only the tips of his toes were still on the ground. He held him there, just held him there so their faces were about six inches apart. Then he said, 'Jonas Jenkins, who do you think is the coward, a man who walks away from a fight he knows he can win, or a man who makes a challenge he knows won't be accepted?' "

"And was that the end of it?" asked Will, unwilling to acknowledge the respect he was feeling for his uncle.

Meg nodded. "Except that Mr. Jenkins hasn't spoken to any of us since."

"I think your ma's doing the right thing, sending him and his wife the extra meat," Will said, shifting the sack to his other shoulder.

"I know, but I'm awful glad I don't have to take it up to the house."

They came out of the woods into a long-neglected field that was dotted with small cedars. Beyond it Will could see the glint of a tin roof.

"There's the house," said Meg, pointing. "Give a holler when you get to the fence. I'll wait for you here."

While he was still a distance away, Will saw an old woman come out of the lean-to that ran the width of the house.

He stopped and shouted, "Hello? Hello!"

The woman turned in his direction and shaded her eyes with her hand. "Who's there?" she called.

For a moment or two, Will was uncertain how to respond. Then he held up the sack and started walking toward her, calling back, "I'm bringing you a rabbit for your dinner. I'm Ella Jones's nephew, Will Page."

They met at the back gate. "Well, I'm pleased to meet

you, Will Page, and I'm right glad for the meat you brought. We—"

"Who's there? Who's out there?" came a loud, peevish voice.

Mrs. Jenkins called back, "It's a young man bringing us a rabbit."

"Well, send him around here so I can see him."

Mrs. Jenkins led the way around to the front of the house. A frail-looking old man with a quilt thrown across his lap sat in a rocking chair on the porch. He leaned forward and squinted at Will.

"Who is this boy?" he asked his wife. "It's nobody I've seen before."

Will climbed the porch steps. "I'm Will Page. I'm from Winchester, but my father was killed in the war, so I've come to live with my Aunt Ella."

"Ella Jones?" the man asked, his eyes narrowing.

Will nodded. "She sent you this rabbit for your dinner," he said, thrusting the sack toward him.

"Rabbit, eh?" he said. Then, turning to his wife he snapped, "Well, you'd better start it cooking if it's going to be ready by noon."

She took the sack and started for the kitchen, and the old man turned his attention back to Will. "So you're Jed Jones's nephew," he said, his eyes narrowing again.

"Aunt Ella and my mother were sisters," Will answered.

Mr. Jenkins gave a bark of a laugh. "I don't blame you for not wanting to admit any kinship to that—"

"He and I don't feel the same about the war, but he's been good to me since I've come here to live," Will interrupted, backing down the porch steps. He hated having to defend his uncle to a man who'd lost two sons in the war, but he knew it would be wrong to stand by and hear him criticized.

"Well, you thank your Aunt Ella and her husband for the rabbit," Mr. Jenkins said, dropping one eyelid in a wink.

At the corner of the house, Will almost collided with Mrs. Jenkins. "Here," she said breathlessly, thrusting a basket into his hands. "Here's something to take back to your aunt."

Inside, nestled on the folded flour sack, were four chicks! Will looked up in surprise.

"The Union foragers thought they'd got my whole flock," the old woman explained, "but I'd stuffed all I could into a burlap sack and hung it in the well. It was dark down there, so they never made a sound, and we've had a few eggs now and then. And just yesterday ol' Biddy hatched out a dozen chicks." She stroked one of them with a gnarled finger. "I think this one's a cockerel."

Will couldn't take his eyes off the tiny balls of fluff. "Thank you," he whispered. "Thank you."

Carefully he carried the basket across the field. "Meg!" he called. "Come see what I've got!"

She came running toward him, her bonnet dangling down her back and a huge bouquet of daisies in her hand. Wordlessly, he held the basket out to her, and before he knew what had happened, he found himself holding the daisies while she sat with the basket on her lap and a tiny chick cradled in her hands. Separated from the others, it began to peep anxiously.

"Come on, Meg, we'd better get them home," urged Will.

She slipped the chick back into the basket and stood up, saying, "I'll carry them."

48

Will felt foolish, trailing along behind her with the daisies, but then he realized that no one would see him, and Aunt Ella would be pleased when he gave her the flowers. But not as pleased as she'd be to have the start of a new flock of chickens!

SIX

"I've a hankering for fish tonight," Uncle Jed said as he sat down at the table the next noon. "Will, why don't you see if you can get us another bass from the millpond?"

Will's stomach churned. What if Hank and the others were there again?

"I'll take him to the river this time," Meg said. And when her father frowned, she leaned forward a little and said urgently, "Please, Pa, let me show him the way!"

"The child deserves an afternoon away from the place, Jed," Aunt Ella said quietly. "She's been working hard since breakfast."

Finally Uncle Jed spoke. "All right. Take him to the river. It'll be less crowded there."

Uncle Jed knew! Meg must have told him. Will felt his face begin to flush. "I'll fish at the pond," he said stiffly.

Uncle Jed looked up. "Good," he said. "Good."

Will didn't know whether he was angry because his uncle had thought he was a coward or because he'd seemed surprised to learn he wasn't. He glanced at Meg. She was staring down at her plate.

"You can show Will the way to the river next time," Uncle Jed told her. "There'll be other fishing trips."

"Oh, let her go along," said Aunt Ella. "She can pick some

of those black raspberries that grow down by the mill. They should be ripe by now." She smiled fondly at her daughter.

"Thanks, Ma," Meg said quietly.

Will had such a knot in his stomach that he could hardly eat. But he managed to chew and swallow everything on his plate. He knew his uncle was watching him, and he didn't want the man to see any sign of the dread he felt. At last the meal was over, and Aunt Ella handed Will a jar for the bait and gave Meg a basket for the berries.

When they were out of earshot, Meg turned to Will in exasperation. "Why did you do that? Why did you say we'd go to the pond when Pa said we could go to the river?"

Patiently, Will explained. "He knew we wanted to go to the river so we wouldn't risk meeting Hank again. I didn't want him to think I'm afraid of Hank and his friends."

"But you *are* afraid, aren't you?"

"I don't want your pa to think I'm a coward," Will said, evading the question. And before Meg could reply, he dashed after a grasshopper that had landed on a rock just ahead of him. He'd been able to talk his way out of trouble with those boys last time, but could he do it again? He was afraid, all right, but he wasn't going to admit it. And he certainly wasn't going to act like it. One coward in this house was enough.

When they had all the bait they needed, Will said, "Why don't you stay here, Meg? You can tell your ma I wanted to go alone."

She shook her head. "Not after she stood up for me with Pa. Anyway, I can't let you go down there and face those bullies all by yourself!"

50

Will gave an empty laugh. "What kind of help do you think you'll be?"

"Well, if they start beating you up, I can run over to the store and get Mr. Riley."

"Who's Mr. Riley?"

"Hank's pa. He owns the store." She grinned. "Hank's plenty scared of him, too, 'cause he's got a terrible temper."

Will didn't answer. He wondered which would be worse—having his cousin rescue him by running for Hank's father or being beaten up. He got Sam's fishing pole from the barn, and they set off.

For once, Meg had little to say. As they walked along the road, Will hoped that they were worrying for nothing. Maybe Hank and his friends wouldn't even be there. He could catch a couple of fish while Meg picked berries, and then they'd go home and he'd have proved to Uncle Jed that he wasn't a coward. Will sighed, realizing that he wouldn't have proved anything at all. He had to face those boys again sometime, and it might as well be today. His muscles tensed at the thought.

When at last the mill came into view ahead of them, Meg whispered, "I don't think they're here."

"They're here," Will said woodenly. "Underneath the sycamore where I fished last time."

Meg caught her breath. "Let's go over by the wheel."

"They'd just come there if we did. You go ahead and pick your berries. I'm going to fish where they are."

"I'm coming with you," Meg said in a small voice.

Will saw Patrick nudge Hank. Hank glanced at them and

then tapped Amos on the shoulder. All three boys stared at them as they approached.

"Have you caught anything big enough to keep, or have you just been throwing the little ones back again?" Will called.

Hank ignored the question. "We was wondering when you was gonna come back, Will-yum Page," he said. "We've got something to ask you about."

"Well, go ahead and ask," said Will, dropping down on one knee to bait his hook. He was relieved to see that Hank and the others were still lounging on the ground.

"You come from Winchester?"

Will nodded without looking up.

"Ever hear of a Charlie Page?"

"Charlie Page?" Will asked dumbly, not turning around. His pulse pounded in his temples and his mouth was dry. How did Hank know about his brother?

And then he heard Meg say, "My ma had a cousin named Charles, but nobody ever called him Charlie."

"I thought maybe this Charlie Page in Winchester was Will-yum's brother," Hank drawled.

"Will's brother was named Peter, but he drowned last summer. He was only eight years old," Meg said mournfully.

Will could hardly believe his ears. He got unsteadily to his feet and tossed his line into the water. Then he took a deep breath and without turning around asked, "What's so important about this Charlie Page?" He was surprised to hear that his voice sounded normal.

"Nothing important about him. He's dead."

Amos broke in eagerly. "My brother, see, he was in the war, and once when the Yankees held Winchester he was on a scouting mission near one of their outposts and he saw this boy, Charlie Page, get shot, and—"

"I don't think Meg wants to hear this story," Hank said. "Have you forgotten that folks in the Jones family didn't want nothing to do with people getting shot in the war? Especially with maybe getting shot themselves," he added.

Will's knuckles were a bloodless white against the fishing pole. He forced himself to say, "*I* want to hear the story. Go pick your berries, Meg."

Meg gave him a long look. Then, without a word, she picked up her basket and left.

Will turned to the fat boy, who seemed to be waiting for permission to continue. "Go on, Amos," he said. He sat down on the bank, his back still toward the others, and concentrated on the cork floating on the water.

"Well, Dan—that's my brother—was supposed to see what he could find out about that Yankee camp. So he was hiding in a ditch watching 'em march back and forth—you know how they meet in the middle, turn 'round, and march back?"

"I've watched sentries lots of times," Will said. "Yankees and Confederates."

"Well, while Dan was trying to figure out the best way to get close to that camp, he saw something move behind a tree there in the field 'tween him and the sentries. It was a boy, and he had him a gray coat hung on a rake and there was this gray hat he'd rigged above it, somehow. Well, what this boy was doing, he was sticking that thing out from behind the tree to taunt those Yankee sentries. He'd stick it out on one side and then on the other, and kind of wiggle it at 'em a little bit.

"Well, Dan, he watched all this for a while, kind of enjoying

53

it, and then all of a sudden he heard a shot—*kerboom!*—and right away another one—*kerboom!* Well, he ducked down in the ditch right fast, but when he didn't hear anything more he real careful raised up and looked out. And he saw that boy layin' there on the ground, dead.

"What he figured happened was, when the boy stuck that dummy soldier out, one of the sentries fired and that startled him and he jerked his rake handle so far back that he came clean out from behind the tree on the other side. And then the other sentry shot him dead. They must have planned it out when they met in the middle, before they turned 'round."

Will's face ached from clenching his jaw so hard. He'd spent the past two years trying to forget that story! He wet his lips with his tongue. "So how did your brother know the boy's name was Charlie Page?" he asked. Then, in a flash of inspiration he added, "Or did you just make that part up?"

"That really was his name, honest!" Amos said. "Two men walking along the road toward town saw it happen and came runnin' over, and Dan heard one of them shout, 'Oh, my God! It's Charlie Page! This is going to kill his mama!' "

Will swallowed hard. "Strange I never heard that story," he said, trying to sound dubious.

"Maybe they tried to keep it quiet so there wouldn't be trouble," said Amos. "It really is a true story. Dan says he'll never forget that man's voice saying, 'Oh, my God! It's Charlie Page! This is going to—' "

"Maybe we didn't hear about it 'cause things like that happened all the time," said Will, interrupting. His heart was pounding so hard that he felt as if his whole body was shaking.

"Or maybe people kind of figured he'd asked for it," said Patrick, speaking for the first time.

"Maybe so," Will said, swallowing hard again.

The boys were silent for a few moments. Then Patrick said, "Tell us some other things that happened in Winchester during the war."

Just then Will felt a tug on his line. As he landed the fish— a bluegill, this time—he wondered what he could tell them. Stories about Yankee soldiers raiding gardens and harrassing citizens and causing careless damage to the homes where they were billeted wouldn't impress these boys. He thought quickly as he strung his cord through the gills and slid the fish back into the water. Then, fastening the end of the cord to an alder branch, he looked straight at Hank.

"Ever see a dead Yankee?" he asked. The older boy's eyes widened, and Will went on. "After the battles they'd be laying all over in front of the courthouse and the bank and on people's porches, with the capes of their uniforms covering up their faces."

Patrick's mouth fell open. "You mean they had battles right in town?"

"There was some fighting in the streets, but the battles weren't in town. They were close enough that we could hear the cannon, though. And sometimes bursts of musket fire, too. Afterward they'd bring the wounded into town. They used churches and other buildings and a lot of homes for hospitals, and when the men died their bodies were carried outside."

"What about our wounded?" Amos asked.

Will's face darkened. "Lots of times the Yankees wouldn't let us onto the battlefields to help our boys till after they'd brought in all their own wounded and buried all their dead. Sometimes it would be more than a day."

"Did you ever go out on a battlefield?" asked Patrick.

"Sure, but not till maybe a week later. My friend Matt and I used to go out with—with some of the older boys and look for uniform buttons and things like that. We'd go into the camps after the armies moved on and look for souvenirs there, too. I found a lot of things. I gave most of them to Matt when I came here."

"But you kept some?"

"Just the buttons."

"I'd sure like to see 'em sometime," said Patrick.

Will didn't answer. He had another bluegill.

"I don't see why you have so much luck," Hank said plaintively.

"Try using grasshoppers for bait instead of worms," Will suggested. "Go ahead and get some out of that jar."

The three boys quickly pulled in their lines and clustered around the jar. When Hank lifted off the handkerchief cover, the insects sprang out like a shower of sparks rising from a fire. He cursed and almost dropped the jar.

Will pretended to be having trouble getting the fish off the hook so the boys wouldn't see his grin. "You have to turn the jar over and shake one out in your hand," he said.

"Aw, we was tired of fishing, anyway," Hank said in disgust. "Say, Will, next time you come, bring some of those buttons you found. I'd like to see 'em."

Will noticed that he wasn't "Will-yum" anymore. "Sure,"

he said, "but I don't know when I'll be able to come again. My uncle keeps me pretty busy around the place."

Hank's lip curled. "The uncle that was afraid of getting shot in the war, you mean?"

Will stood up and looked Hank straight in the eye. "I don't want you to mention my uncle again. His not going to war doesn't have anything to do with me."

There was a long silence. Then Hank gave a quick nod. "Well, bring the buttons when you come."

"I'll try to remember," Will said, slinging the string of fish over his shoulder and picking up the pole. "And see if you don't have better luck with grasshoppers."

Meg met him at the road. Her basket was nearly full of berries, and her mouth was stained purple. There was a long juicy smear above one eye, too. She glanced over her shoulder at the three boys under the sycamore.

"Do you think they'll follow us?" she asked nervously.

"Nah. They won't follow us."

"How can you be so sure?" she asked, walking faster.

Will grinned. "'Cause we're friends now—sort of. They invited me to fish with them again." Then he grew serious. "But how did you know what was coming when they asked me about Charlie?"

Meg shifted the heavy berry basket to her other arm. "Well, after we got back from the mill pond last time, I asked Pa why a sentry would kill a boy, and he told me the whole story."

"I guess Doc Martin had told your ma."

Meg nodded. "But she and Pa already knew. You see, Pa heard that story down at the mill, when Amos's brother came home after he was wounded more than a year ago."

"But they never told you, even after I came here?"

Meg shook her head. "Ma just said not to ask you questions about your family, 'cause it would make you sad. But I didn't pay any attention, 'cause it doesn't make me sad to talk about Beth. I guess I should have listened to her, though. I'm sorry, Will."

"Well, I'm not! Not anymore, at least. If you hadn't asked me about Charlie that day, you'd never have known to throw those boys off the track the way you did."

Meg was silent for a moment. Then she said, "I don't blame you for not wanting to talk about it."

Will's words came in a rush. "You see, back home, whenever people saw me they were reminded of what had happened because they knew I was Charlie's brother. I could tell they were thinking about it and feeling sorry for me even when they didn't say anything, and it was awful. The one good thing about coming here was that nobody knew. That people wouldn't be thinking of Charlie's death every time they saw me, and that I wouldn't constantly be reminded of it." Turning toward Meg, he added, "I just hope those boys believed what you said."

Meg grinned. "I'm sure they did. I don't think you have to worry about people around here connecting you with the Charlie Page story. And if anybody else does wonder about it, one of those boys will set them straight."

"Thanks for helping me out, Meg. . . . I'll always remember Charlie, but I want to forget about the way he died."

Meg nodded. "Pa said Dan told them he'd got used to seeing men killed in battle, but he didn't think he'd ever forget seeing a schoolboy shot or hearing that man's voice when he said,

58

'This is going to kill his mama.' " She paused a moment and then said quietly, "I hope you don't believe that's why your ma died."

Will walked a few steps in silence. Then he said, "She never really got over what happened, but it didn't kill her. I think it was losing Betsy and Eleanor that made her feel she didn't have any reason for living."

"She still had you."

"I guess I wasn't enough," he said, struggling to keep his voice steady.

Meg said quietly, "She was sick, Will. She died because she was sick."

"Doc Martin said she'd lost the will to live."

"But that's different from making up your mind to die 'cause you don't have anything to live for. My ma would never do that, and I don't think yours would have, either," Meg said firmly.

They didn't talk much the rest of the way home, but it was an easy silence. Will noticed in surprise that they were walking in step. That had sometimes happened when he was walking with Matt, but he'd never imagined it would happen when he was walking with a girl! But then, Meg was an unusual girl.

SEVEN

"Load those charred posts on the slide and pull them over to the pasture while I get my tools. We'll replace some of those rotting posts today."

Will hurried to do what his uncle asked, glad for a change in their afternoon routine. They met at the fence.

"How do we get the old posts out?" Will asked.

"Like this," his uncle said, digging in his spade.

Will's spirits fell. It would take forever to dig out all the old fence posts!

"Now, watch," said his uncle after he had dug out several spadefuls of dirt. He looped a short length of chain around the exposed base of the post and fastened it loosely. Then he passed a fence rail through the chain next to the post, twisted it tight, and rested the side of the rail on the ground at the edge of the hole.

Of course! Will thought. He'd use that as a lever!

Uncle Jed put his weight on the end of the rail and lifted the post up several inches. "Slide the chain farther down now," he directed.

Will scrambled to do as he was asked. This wasn't going to take as long as he had feared!

Near midafternoon, they heard a call. "Will! Hey, Will!"

Will looked up and saw Hank coming down the lane. Surprised, he waved.

"The mail stage brought a letter from Ohio, and Pa sent me over with it," Hank called, waving an envelope.

As Hank walked toward them, Uncle Jed turned to Will. "We're going to keep right on working, you hear?"

Will nodded, wondering why. He didn't look up when he heard Hank walking through the tall grass to the fence, but out of the corner of his eye he could see him holding out the envelope.

"Here's your letter." When Uncle Jed didn't turn around, Hank stood there awkwardly and then said, "I guess it's from Sam and Enos." But still Uncle Jed just went on working.

Finally, in desperation, the boy burst out, "Don't you want your letter, Mr. Jones?"

At that, Uncle Jed turned. "Oh, were you speaking to me?" he asked, reaching out for the letter.

All at once, Will understood. His uncle had refused to respond until Hank called him by name! Well, he'd tricked Hank into saying "Mr. Jones," but he'd never trick him into saying "Uncle Jed."

"It was right neighborly of you to bring this all the way out here, Hank," Uncle Jed said as he tore open the envelope.

"Pa said you'd been lookin' for it for a while and I should bring it on out," Hank mumbled.

"Well, you tell your pa I'm much obliged," he said. He read the letter quickly, then handed it to Will. "Take this in to your aunt. She's been waiting a long time to hear from those boys." Then, turning back to Hank, he said, "It was good talking to you after all this time."

Will started off toward the house and Hank followed. "How come it's been so long since you and my uncle saw each other?" he asked, pausing to let Hank catch up.

Hank looked sheepish and said, "Oh, we seen each other often enough. We just hadn't talked." Then, quickly changing the subject, he asked, "Say, Will, I was wondering if maybe I could see those buttons of yours."

"Sure," Will agreed cheerfully. "I'll show you my father's saber, too."

A moment later, Aunt Ella was poring over the letter and the boys were in the attic. Will took the saber and the leather pouch from their nail on the wall. He slipped the drawstring of the pouch around his wrist and carefully drew the long, curved blade from its scabbard. Even in the dim light of the attic, it gleamed.

Hank was properly awed. "They gave my pa a bayonet for on his musket, but he never had no sword. Your pa ever kill anybody with that there sword?" he asked as Will slid the saber back into its scabbard and hung it on the wall.

Will turned around. "Of course!" he said in surprise. "Didn't yours ever kill anybody with his bayonet?"

"Nah," said Hank.

"Well, my father killed lots of Yankees with his saber and even more with his revolver." As soon as the words were out, Will regretted their boastful tone. It didn't seem quite right to brag about how many men Papa'd killed. "Let me show you the buttons," he said quickly, emptying the contents of the pouch onto the floor.

Hank dropped to his knees. "Look at 'em all!" he said, picking up a button embossed with an eagle and the letter *C*.

"That's a Yankee button," said Will. "I found that one on the battlefield at Kernstown." He thought of how he and his friend Matt had begged Charlie to take them along to look for battle souvenirs.

"If it's Yankee, how come it's got a *C* on it?"

"For 'Cavalry,' " Will explained, sorting through his collection. "See this one with the *I*? It's off a Yankee infantry officer's uniform."

"How d'you know he was an officer?"

" 'Cause except for the artillery, Yankee enlisted men just had the number of their regiment on their buttons," Will said. Then, seeing Hank's scowl, he quickly added, "You'd know all this stuff, too, if there'd been any big battles near here.

And if you'd had a brother like Charlie to teach it to you."

"A brother like Charlie," Hank repeated slowly. "So Charlie Page *was* your brother!"

Will was devastated. How could he have been so stupid!

"Why'd you lie to us down at the pond that day?"

"I just didn't want to talk about it," Will said through clenched teeth.

"So you sat there and listened to Amos tell the whole story and pretended you'd never heard it before?"

Will glared at Hank. "I don't want to talk about it now, either. Do you want to see the rest of these buttons, or not?" To his relief, Hank shrugged and picked up a button showing a woman warrior with her foot resting on a vanquished foe.

"Which side's this one from?"

Will was amazed that Hank didn't recognize the Virginia State Seal. "That's from a Virginia militia uniform. Lots of men that volunteered at the beginning of the war went in their militia uniforms. My father did."

"Your pa *volunteered*?" Hank asked in disbelief.

"Of course! It was his duty!"

Hank quickly changed the subject. "Look at this," he said, reaching into his pocket and drawing out an oval buckle. A bullet hole obliterated the first letter, but the other two—*VM*—could still be read.

Will took it. "A Yankee belt plate," he said, imagining a Confederate sharpshooter fixing his sight on the glint of the volunteer militia man's shiny buckle. "Where'd you get this?"

"Tom, my brother, he swapped for it when they had a truce at the battleline. Cost him a pipe he'd carved from a laurel root."

63

"Your brother swapped with a Yankee?" Will asked in disbelief.

"Shucks, he was just another farm boy. Gave Tom some bacon, too. First meat he'd had in weeks."

Will handed back the buckle and swept the scattered buttons into a pile. He said stiffly, "My family never had anything to do with Yankees no matter how long we'd been without meat."

"Why not?" Hank asked in surprise. "How could filling your belly with extra vittles help the enemy?"

Will put the last of the buttons into the pouch and tightened the drawstring. "It wouldn't have helped the enemy," he said, "but it would have hurt us. It would have hurt our pride."

Hank was quiet for a minute. "Pride's pretty important to you, ain't it?" he said at last.

Will stood up. "It's all I have left," he said.

Hank got to his feet, too, and gave Will a long, calculating look. Then he turned to leave, saying over his shoulder, "I'll be watching for you down at the millpond, Will-yum Page."

From the window, Will watched Hank cross the yard. For a while, he'd thought they might be friends. But that was before Hank found out he'd lied about Charlie. And before he'd acted like such a prig about Hank's brother and the Yankee soldier.

"I was surprised Hank Riley hung around so long after he handed over that letter," Uncle Jed said that night at supper.

Will wished his uncle hadn't reminded him of Hank's visit. "He wanted to see the uniform buttons my friend Matt and I collected around Winchester. I showed him Papa's saber, too," he explained.

Meg sighed. "I wish I could have seen all that."

Will looked up in surprise. He hadn't thought a girl would be interested in such things. "I'll show them to you when we're through supper," he said.

"Wouldn't mind seeing 'em myself," said Uncle Jed.

So after the dishes had been washed and dried, Will brought down the pouch and saber. He drew the saber from its scabbard and laid it on the table, pretending he didn't see his uncle's outstretched hand. Uncle Jed picked it up and ran a finger along the finely sharpened blade. "Never saw one of these before," he admitted.

Meg's eyes were wide. "Did your pa really kill men with that? It must be terrible to see the face of somebody you have to kill!" She shuddered.

Uncle Jed slid the saber back into its scabbard. "Yes, I guess it's easier to fire your musket at somebody that's wearing a different color uniform. Or just to aim your cannon in the general direction of the other side."

Will felt a flood of anger sweep through him. "There's times a man can't take the easy way out," he said, glaring at his uncle.

His uncle's dark eyes met his and held. "That's right, Will. A man has to do what he believes is right."

Will looked away, confused. Did Uncle Jed really believe he'd done the right thing when he refused to fight? He was glad when Meg broke the strained silence.

"Can we see the buttons now?" she asked.

He emptied the pouch onto the table. "Each one is different," he said. "I gave my friend Matt all my duplicates so he could swap 'em for ones he doesn't have."

"Which ones are Yankee and which ones are Johnny Reb?" asked Meg, leaning forward.

How Will wished his cousin would say "Confederate"! He sorted the buttons into two piles, muttering under his breath as he worked: "Thirteenth Georgia . . . Seventh Maine . . . Ohio Volunteer Militia . . . Twenty-sixth Massachusetts. . . ."

"And just think, a man probably died right where you found every one of those buttons," Meg said when he had finished.

Will had never thought of it quite that way before. He wished his cousin hadn't said it.

"What I don't understand is," she went on, "why you have so many more Yankee buttons. If so many more Yankees were killed, how could they win the war?"

"Easy," said Uncle Jed, pushing his chair away from the table. "They had more men to waste." The door slammed shut behind him.

Meg helped Will gather up the buttons and put them back in the pouch. "Thank you for showing me your collection," she said politely when they had finished. Then she went up to her attic room and closed the door quietly behind her.

Will stared down at the leather pouch. "I think I'll get rid of these," he said at last.

Aunt Ella reached over and laid her hand on his. "No, Will. Don't do that. That collection is part of your past, and you have little enough left to remember it by."

Back in his room, Will whispered, "Aunt Ella's right. I don't have much to remember the past by." His hand lingered on the saber as he hung the belt on its nail, then moved to the family Bible on the table beneath the window. Idly, he turned to the family record pages. In the waning light he could just make out the last two entries in his mother's writing: Elizabeth Anne Page, born June 1, 1855, died August 18, 1864; Eleanor Jeanne Page, born July 3, 1857, died August 19, 1864. He flipped back to the page where he'd recorded his mother's death. Why? Why did she have to die?

The weight of the leather pouch made its drawstring cut into his wrist, and Will pulled it over his hand and tossed it onto the table. He thought of his cousin's words: "A man probably died right where you found every one of those buttons." Had some other boy walked along the Middletown Road where his father's unit was ambushed and looked for buttons and belt plates to collect?

Will threw himself face down on his bed and relived the night three years before when he had learned of Papa's death. Lizzy had come upstairs to tell him and Charlie that their mother wanted to see them. In the parlor, a handsome blond cavalry officer rose and came to meet them. Mama was standing at the window, her back ramrod stiff and her hands clenched at her sides, so the young major introduced himself. And then, as gently as he could, he told them how Papa had fallen in battle.

Will had stared down at the man's dusty boots and tried not to listen to his words. All he remembered now was what the man had said as he left: "Your father was a brave soldier. He died facing the enemy."

Rolling over onto his back, Will stared at the dark rectangle of the attic window. His father was brave. His father had faced the enemy, but Uncle Jed had run away from his own side— from the conscription teams that simply wanted him to meet his responsibilities. "I can never respect a man who refused to fight for his country, no matter how good a man he seems to be in peacetime," Will said aloud.

It was a long time before he fell asleep.

After the morning chores were done, Uncle Jed and Will set to work again on the fence repairs. Remembering his decision of the night before, Will maintained an awkward silence. Finally, to cover his discomfort, he began to whistle. It wasn't until he noticed the set of his uncle's mouth that he realized he'd been whistling "When Johnny Comes Marching Home." In a flash, Will realized Uncle Jed thought he'd chosen that tune to provoke him! And then, with a strange feeling of excitement in his chest, he began to sing the words quietly under his breath, watching his uncle out of the corner of his eye.

The big man's hands continued to ease the rotting posts out of the ground and replace them with new ones. And before long, he began to hum along with Will!

Will began the last verse. He wasn't surprised his uncle didn't know the words the Southern soldiers had sung to the lively tune.

> *"In eighteen hundred and sixty-five*
> *(Hurrah, hurrah!)*
> *We all thanked God we were alive. . . . "*

His voice faltered, and he bit his lip.

Uncle Jed straightened up and looked across the pasture toward the mountains. "Too many men aren't alive anymore because of that war," he said at last. "And that song doesn't mention when Johnny came hobbling home on one leg and a crutch, or when he didn't come home at all and his family never knew where he was buried. You know where your pa's buried, lad?"

"Near where he fell," Will answered grudgingly. Then, quoting the young major, he added, "He died facing the enemy."

Turning toward Will, Uncle Jed said, "I've faced enemies, too—the enemies of us all. Hunger. Illness. Grief. And hatred. But I've never faced my own countrymen as enemies. A man isn't my enemy just 'cause he believes different than I do."

Will looked at his uncle in amazement. It almost sounded as if he were criticizing Papa! "Papa's enemies weren't his own countrymen! His country was the Confederacy, and he was fighting alongside his Confederate countrymen against their Yankee enemies!"

"Your Pa did what he believed was right when he went to war. And I did what I believed was right when I didn't go."

Will didn't know what to think. He bent to slide the chain lower on the rotting post. As his uncle rested his weight on the lever Will asked, "Would you go to war to protect your country against another country?"

"If it meant staying free, I would."

"Well, my father's country was fighting against another country in order to stay free."

Uncle Jed straightened up and lifted his worn straw hat to wipe the sweat off his forehead. "How do you figure that?"

"Well, Virginia and the other states seceded and formed the Confederacy so they could be free to make the laws that suited their own people."

Uncle Jed grunted as he took a new post from Will and stood it upright in the hole. "So they could be free to keep other people as slaves, you mean. Free to buy and sell other people like livestock."

Will squirmed uncomfortably. "They wanted each state to be free to decide whether to have slaves or not."

"Looks to me like all the states that seceded had already decided to have them," Uncle Jed observed.

Will didn't have any answer to that. Thinking fast, he said, "A lot of men who didn't own slaves fought in the war, you know. Like Hank's father and brother, and Mr. Jenkins' sons, and your other neighbors. Why would they have been in the war unless they were fighting for states' rights?"

Uncle Jed snorted. "Mr. Riley and Tom fought because the conscriptors got 'em. The Jenkins boys heard how Stonewall Jackson sent the Yankees packing at Manassas and joined the army to find adventure. The rest of 'em were fighting for Virginia."

"I guess you didn't love Virginia enough to fight for her," Will said smugly.

His uncle pushed his hat higher on his sweating forehead. "That's the Virginia I love," he said, swinging his arm in a wide arc that took in the woods and hills and the mountains in the distance. Then he scooped up a handful of small clods. "And this is the Virginia I love." He crumbled the dirt and watched it trickle between his fingers. "And I didn't want any part of bloodying Virginia's soil."

As his uncle turned to pick up the next post Will felt a sense of relief that the conversation was over. He didn't know quite what to make of the man.

70

EIGHT

"When I went in the store yesterday to mail your letter to the twins, the men were talking about repairing the mill," Will announced at breakfast a few days later.

"They say when they plan to start?" his uncle asked.

Will nodded. "They're meeting there this morning."

"After you check the trap line, we'll go on down. I'll gather up some tools for us."

It was nearly midmorning when they arrived at the mill. A stack of fresh lumber was piled by the waterwheel, and half a dozen men stood near it. No one spoke as Uncle Jed and Will approached.

"Thought you might need some extra hands on this job," Uncle Jed said, pushing back his hat.

The men glanced quickly at one another and then looked at the miller. But before he could speak, a young man who looked vaguely familiar to Will stepped forward. His eyes traveled insolently from Uncle Jed's hat to his dusty boots and back up to his face. "Don't guess we need *your* help, but I reckon we could use the boy," he said.

Will's heart almost stood still.

Uncle Jed gazed levelly into the younger man's eyes. "Well, Tom, let me know if you change your mind," he said quietly.

It was Tom who looked away first, dropping his gaze to Will. "Run on over to the store and tell Pa we need them nails now," he said.

Why, Tom was Hank's brother! Will swallowed hard, realizing that Uncle Jed had already turned toward home and now Tom and the other men were waiting to see what he would do.

"My—my uncle needs me. I—I'd better go with him."

Tom's lip curled in derision. "Suit yourself," he said.

Will could feel six pairs of eyes on him as he left. Uncle Jed was passing the spring when Will caught up to him. For a few minutes, neither spoke. Then Uncle Jed said, "You could have stayed. It might have made things easier for you in the long run."

"I didn't want to stay," Will said shortly. He was seething with indignation. Tom Riley had no right to treat Uncle Jed like that, even if he hadn't been in the war.

———————

Will listened for the sounds of hammering as he approached the mill a week later. He'd wanted Meg to show him the way to the river that afternoon, but he was afraid that if he didn't go to the pond, Uncle Jed would think it was because of what had happened when they volunteered to help repair the mill. And he'd be right. Will could still feel the men's eyes boring into his back. He dreaded meeting them again, especially Hank's brother Tom.

His spirits rose when he didn't hear any hammering as he drew near the mill. Maybe they'd finished the repairs! But then he saw the little knot of men clustered around the waterwheel.

At first, they didn't seem to notice him, but when he stood up to cast, he saw the miller glance in his direction. For a few minutes Will kept his eyes fixed on the cork floating on the still water, but then he slowly lifted them and saw the men talking among themselves. Suddenly Tom Riley broke away from the group and headed toward his father's store, his body stiff with anger. Then, as the others nodded, Mr. Brown left the group and began walking around the pond toward Will.

Puzzled, Will concentrated on the cork again.

"Having any luck?" the man called as he approached.

"No, sir," said Will. "Not yet." And not the last three or four times he'd gone there, either.

Giving Will a friendly clap on the shoulder the miller said, "Well, you ain't been here very long."

Just then, Will's cork bobbed and went under. He jerked the line and quickly landed a bluegill.

"Couple more of them, and you'll be having a fish supper," said the man.

"Yessir," Will said, skillfully working the hook from the fish's mouth. Then, feeling he should say more, he asked, "How's the mill coming along?"

The man studied his fingernails for a few moments and then sighed. "Not so well. Oh, we've got the rotted boards replaced," he said, following Will's glance toward the patchwork of new and aged boards on the mill's exterior. "It's the works that's troubling us now. Can't seem to get that fool wheel turning no matter what we do."

"That's a real problem."

"So it is," the man said. Then he leaned forward. "But, say—there's something you could do to help."

"Something *I* could do? What do you mean?"

"Your uncle worked for a miller over in Madison County when he was a young man, and I'd like him to take a look at the millworks for me. Would you tell him that?"

Will felt a tug on his line. "Another bluegill," he said, glad for the chance to collect his thoughts before he answered. Uncle Jed had said to let him know if they changed their minds, but he'd said it to Tom. Tossing his line in again, Will turned to the miller. "I think you'd better send Tom Riley with that message, sir."

"So that's the way it's going to be." The miller sighed. Then, standing up, he added, "Can't say that I blame you, though."

Will watched Mr. Brown walk back around the pond and join the other men. Again he saw them look in his direction and then nod their heads. Finally, they all set off toward Riley's store. Will sat for what he thought was at least another hour before he gathered up his two bluegills and started home.

"Mr. Brown said he'd like you to take a look at the millworks," Will told his uncle that night at supper.

"Did you tell him I would?"

"I told him he'd better send Tom Riley out here to ask you."

"Tom's a stubborn young man," Uncle Jed said slowly. "I doubt that Luke Brown can get him to do that."

Will stared down at his plate. Now he'd ruined everything. And he was just trying to do what he thought Uncle Jed would want.

A little later, while Meg sat on the porch step with the coffee mill on her lap, grinding buckwheat for the next morning's breakfast gruel, Will carefully filled the oil lamps and trimmed their wicks. Suddenly he spoke. "I don't see that Tom Riley has much right to look down on your pa for not fighting since he only went to war because the conscriptors got him." And since he fraternized with the enemy, he added silently, remembering the shiny buckle Tom had gotten by swapping with a Yankee.

Meg shrugged. "He probably hates to think that Pa was smarter than he was about avoiding the conscriptors."

"Maybe so," Will said. He sighed, wondering if the miller would be able to convince Tom to come and ask for Uncle Jed's help.

NINE

It was almost a week later when Will saw Tom Riley coming across the pasture to where he and Uncle Jed were working on the fence. When Tom reached them, he stood as if at attention, not meeting their eyes.

"I have a message for Jed Jones from Luke Brown, the miller," he announced. "He needs help fixing the millworks." Then he turned on his heel and retraced his steps as grasshoppers exploded from the tall grass in front of him.

Uncle Jed tamped earth around the post that Will held in place. Then he straightened up and mopped his sweating brow with his handkerchief. "Well, looks like Tom finally got around to delivering that message."

Will nodded, almost weak with relief.

Uncle Jed went on. "We'll go on in there tomorrow and act as if none of that unpleasantness ever happened."

Will nodded again, silently resolving to avoid Tom whenever he could.

But when they reached the mill early the next day, Will

realized he needn't have been concerned about avoiding Tom—he was nowhere to be seen.

"Glad to see you, Jed," the miller said, shaking hands as several of the other men echoed his greeting. "And you, young man," he said, turning to Will, "have you come to help or to catch some more of them bluegills?"

Before Will could answer, his uncle replied, "He's come to watch. It's a good chance for a youngster to learn something."

Will followed the men into the cool, dusty building and down the plank stairs to a dark, earth-floored room filled with the machinery that turned the millstone on the floor above. When his eyes had adjusted to the dimness of the wheel pit, he saw from the new wood that parts of the gears had been painstakingly repaired. Then he looked up at the complicated system of belts and pulleys that turned the gears and saw that all of the belts were new.

Following his gaze, the miller explained. "One of the Yankee foraging parties was a mite unhappy that I didn't have any flour or cornmeal for them, and they took it out on me by ruining the millworks. Slashed the belts with their sabers and banged the notches off the gears with my own ax. But I guess I was lucky. If it hadn't been the middle of a wet spell, they'd have burned me to the ground."

"Looks like you did a right good job on these gears," Uncle Jed commented as he ran a hand over the nearest one.

"What I haven't been able to manage for the life of me, though, is to get those new belts to turn them. They just slip right off the pulley," said the miller. "I never had this kind of problem before."

Uncle Jed nodded, letting his gaze run from ceiling to floor and from wall to wall, studying the arrangement of gear wheels and pulleys. Finally he spoke. "I think I see the problem. Shouldn't take too long to set things right."

He set to work, adjusting the pairs of pulleys and making sure they were absolutely parallel. Will watched, fascinated, until the miller's wife called them to dinner.

Will followed the men up the steps and out into the brightness of noonday. A cloth-covered table had been set up in the shade, and his mouth began to water as the smell of fried chicken reached his nostrils. And then he saw the bowls of steaming mashed potatoes, green beans cooked with great chunks of salt pork, and corn pudding. This was more food than he'd seen at one time for years!

Noticing his reaction to the heavily laden table, one of the younger men grinned. "The Yankees may have messed up the millworks for ol' man Brown, but earlier in the war he did a lot of milling for them, and the government finally paid him. That's how he can afford to fix the mill now, and how his missus can set a table like this one. He just bought her a cow and a whole flock of laying hens, too."

"Mr. Brown worked for the Yankees?" Will asked in dismay.

"Son, when armed men tell you to grind grain, you grind it."

Will didn't like to think of Mr. Brown working for the enemy. But he had to admit the miller hadn't had much choice.

Mrs. Brown heaped Will's plate high with food. "Now, will you be having lemonade or milk with that?" she asked.

His unbelieving eyes turned toward the two pitchers, one filled with gold-flecked juice and floating chips of ice and the other with frothy milk.

Smiling at his indecision, the plump, pleasant-faced woman poured him a glass of lemonade. "Drink this now and have some milk with dessert." Then, leaning closer, she whispered, "I've made cherry pies."

Will took the glass and managed to thank her. Then he sank to the ground and began to eat. The taste of that first bite of crisply fried chicken brought him a rush of memories. Memories of a time when food like this was taken for granted. Memories of the family dinner hour with Callie's succulent meals, Charlie's wisecracks, his little sisters' giggles, and his parents' quiet conversation.

"Why, you've hardly touched your dinner! Aren't you feeling well?" Mrs. Brown's concerned voice interrupted his reverie.

"Stomach's shrunk, no doubt," said Uncle Jed. "Give him a little time for it to stretch."

Later, when Will carried his empty plate and glass over to the table, Mrs. Brown beamed and cut him a thick wedge of pie. "Everything was delicious, ma'am," he said, watching her fill his glass with milk.

"I'm glad your stomach stretched enough that you could enjoy it," she said, smiling.

The heavy meal made Will sleepy. He yawned as he followed the men down into the dark wheel pit, but its coolness revived him. He watched Uncle Jed work, impressed by his careful, confident approach to the job and by the other men's obviously increasing respect. Wasn't there anything his uncle didn't know how to do?

At last Uncle Jed straightened up. "That look about right to you, Luke?" he asked.

"Sure does," replied the miller. "Let's try 'er out. Will, you go raise the sluice gate."

Will hurried up the stairs and dashed out the door. Just above the mill wheel, a wooden gate had been lowered to divert the water from the mill race directly to the pond. How was he supposed to raise the gate so the water could drop down onto the huge waterwheel? The control must be inside, he realized.

Will ran back into the mill. Against the wall was a wooden lever. He released its T-shaped handle and used all his strength to push it down, feeling the tremor of the gate inching its way up. He locked the lever into position and stood at the narrow window, watching the stream of water fall onto the waterwheel. The huge wheel gave a shudder and slowly began to turn. Gradually it picked up speed, and above its creaking, Will heard the steady slapping sound of the belts as they whirled around the pulleys, the hum of the turning gears, and the triumphant shouts from the men in the wheel pit. Uncle Jed had done it!

Will had to see for himself. He raced down the stairs, passing the men as they were hurrying up them. Alone in the wheel pit, he watched the millworks in operation. Uncle Jed had known just what to do, he marveled. At last he tore himself away from the hypnotic spell of the machinery and ran up to the floor above where the miller was emptying a sack of wheat into the funnellike hopper above the millstone.

"Come here, boy," the miller called. "Come over here and watch!" He turned a lever and lowered the top millstone so that it would grind the grain against the bottom one. The whole building vibrated as the giant stone began to turn.

The miller's helper headed for the stairs, and Mr. Brown turned to Will. "I want you to go with him," he said, gesturing toward the young man, "and bring me the first sack of flour."

Will and the miller's helper watched the flour sift through the mesh bolting cloths after it came down the chute from the floor above. "Where'd Mr. Brown get the grain?" Will asked. He had to shout to make himself heard over the noise of the machinery.

"From Ohio," was the answering shout.

Imagine having to ship grain to Virginia! Will thought. Before the war, the Shenandoah Valley had produced so much wheat its mills ran twenty-four hours a day. But then General Sheridan and his Yankee troops had ravaged the Valley, destroying the crops, burning the mills, and—

"You look angry," shouted the miller's helper.

"I was thinking about how the Yankees burned the mills in the Valley," Will shouted back.

The miller's helper shrugged. "That's the way it is in wartime. I was with our cavalry in Pennsylvania when we burned Chambersburg. Houses, shops, hotels—we sent them all afire. Burned most of the city."

Will stared at him. He looked like a perfectly ordinary young man, but he'd just admitted to burning people's homes! At least Sheridan had ordered that the homes be spared when he sent his army to plunder the Valley, though the skeletal chimneys scattered along the pike showed that the fires had sometimes gotten out of hand.

Will turned to watch the flour pouring from the chute and tried not to think about Confederate soldiers burning Chambersburg. When the sack was filled, the miller's helper sewed it shut with long stitches and knotted the string at the end. Will shouldered the sack and climbed the stairs.

When he reached the top, the miller called to him. "Bring that on over here!" he said. Then, taking it from Will, he held it out to Uncle Jed. "This first sack of flour goes to the man who made it all possible!" he said grandly.

Amid the cheers of the other men, Uncle Jed took the sack. "I'm much obliged for this," he said. "And I know Ella's going to be right happy to have it."

As Will started out the door with his uncle, he heard the miller say, "Don't the rest of you leave yet—there'll be a sack of flour for each of you, too."

Outside, Mrs. Brown called to them. "Take these leftovers in case you get hungry on the way home," she said, handing Will a napkin-covered basket. "There's butter and eggs for your aunt, too." Then, brushing off his thanks, she hurried back to the house.

As they headed toward the road, Will saw a tall figure standing under the sycamore watching the water turn the creaking mill wheel. It was Tom. Uncle Jed raised his hand in a silent greeting, and after a moment's pause, Tom grudgingly returned the salute. Will thought he saw the hint of a smile under his uncle's bushy beard.

A few minutes later they stopped at the roadside spring, and while Uncle Jed drank a dipperful of the cold water, Will lifted the napkin from the basket and peeked inside. Besides a dozen eggs and the round of butter wrapped in a damp cloth, there was enough fried chicken for supper, and a whole pie! He grinned, thinking how surprised and pleased Aunt Ella and Meg would be.

"Not bad wages for a day's work," Uncle Jed commented as he shouldered the sack of flour and they started off again.

" 'The laborer is worthy of his hire,' " Will said, wondering if his uncle would recognize the biblical quotation.

TEN

"Will, I want you to see if the miller's wife will trade you butter for that rabbit you got this morning," Aunt Ella said. "I'd rather do without meat than butter, now that I've gotten used to having it again."

"Well, with any luck, you won't have to do without meat for supper. I'm going squirrel hunting this afternoon," announced Uncle Jed.

"I'll try to catch some bluegills after I see Mrs. Brown, in case you don't have any luck," Will said, leaving the table.

As he walked down the dusty road, Will thought of how his uncle had fixed the millworks the week before. He hoped people would be so glad to have the mill grinding again that they'd forget Uncle Jed hadn't fought the Yankees.

When he knocked on the door at the miller's house, Mrs. Brown welcomed him warmly and said she'd be happy to trade butter for any rabbits he'd bring. "Now, don't forget to come back for the butter when you're through fishing," she said as he finished the apple pie and milk she'd insisted that he have.

"I won't," he assured her, adding shyly, "I think that's the best pie I ever ate."

"Oh, go on, now," she said, pleased.

Will heard the creak of the waterwheel as he approached the mill, and then he saw Amos lounging on the grass and Hank leaning against the sycamore across the pond.

"Hey!" he called, waving.

Hank waved back. He had something white in his hand. "You've got a letter," he called.

Will hurried around the pond. But when he reached for the letter, Hank stuffed it in his pocket! Without a word, Will turned and picked up his bait jar. Holding it upside down, he shook out a grasshopper. He put the insect on the hook, managing to keep his hand steady, and cast his line out into the pond.

"Don't you want your letter?" asked Amos.

"Sure I want it," Will said.

"Why don't you come and get it then?" asked Hank.

Without looking around, Will said, "I reckon you'll give it to me when you're ready to." He clenched his teeth and kept his eyes on the cork floating on the still surface of the water. Now and then he brushed the gnats away from his face. Who would be writing him a letter? Could it be from Matt? His fingers tingled with the urge to rip the envelope from Hank's pocket.

"Who do you think the letter's from?" Amos asked.

Will shrugged.

"Well," Amos said, "it can't be from Charlie Page. He's dead."

Will threw his fishing pole to the ground and jumped to his

feet. In three steps he was facing Hank. "You asked me why I lied about Charlie? That's why! So nobody would—would taunt me about his death. So I could remember him alive instead of being reminded about the way he died."

Hank looked embarrassed. "We thought it was because you were ashamed of him."

Ashamed of Charlie? "Of course I wasn't ashamed of Charlie! He was the best brother anybody could have!" Shaking with anger, Will turned his back on the other boys and picked up his pole. Sitting on the bank again, he fixed his attention on the floating cork and tried to ignore the pounding in his temples.

Finally, after what seemed like hours, Hank came and sat beside him on the bank. The corner of the envelope was sticking out of his pocket. It took all of Will's self-control not to make a grab for it.

"These bugs sure are bad today," Hank complained, waving the letter in front of his face like a fan.

"Fishing's not much better," said Will.

"Well, you can stay here if you want to, but I'm going over to the store," Hank said at last, slapping at a large fly that lit on his knee. Stuffing the envelope back into his pocket, he motioned for Amos to follow him, and the two boys sauntered off.

Will felt a blinding flash of rage. If only Hank weren't so much bigger than he was! But he'd get even with him for this somehow.

All through that long, muggy afternoon Will sat by the pond, brushing away the troublesome gnats. Why weren't the fish biting? And how long should he wait before he went over to the store and asked Mr. Riley for the letter?

Suddenly Will sensed that something was different. It was a moment or so before he realized that he no longer heard the creaking of the mill wheel. And then he saw how long the shadows were. It was later than he'd thought! Quickly he pulled his line from the water—noticing with disgust that his bait was gone—and stuck the barb of the hook into the cork. Emptying the remaining grasshoppers from the jar, he hurried toward the store. Mr. Riley was almost ready to lock up when Will got there.

"I—I came for my letter, Mr. Riley," he said, panting.

"Your letter? Didn't Hank give you that letter?"

"No, sir."

"He didn't bring it to you over at the pond?"

Will didn't know what to say. Embarrassed, he shifted his weight from one foot to the other.

After a long moment the storekeeper turned away, swearing under his breath. He went behind the counter and took a handful of letters from a box on one of the shelves. Sorting through them quickly, he found the one addressed to Will. Mr. Riley handed it to him and said grimly, "You can be sure that Hank will hear from me about this."

Will didn't recognize the handwriting on the envelope, but with a pang of disappointment he knew at once that it wasn't Matt's. He turned the envelope over and saw Doc Martin's return address written on the flap. Why would Doc Martin be writing to him? It was all he could do to wait until he was outside before he tore the envelope open and began to read.

August 10, 1865

Dear Will,

When I left you at your aunt's farm in June, I found myself questioning the wisdom of that arrangement. Not because of your feelings about your uncle's refusal to fight for the Confederacy, but because I am sure that your dear mother had no idea of the hardships you would have to face there.

My older sister, a widow, has come to live with me, so now I can offer you a proper home. I am sure your dear mother would not, under the circumstances, blame us for not continuing to follow her instructions for your care.

You are a fine boy, Will, and I would be proud to raise you as my son. But you must make your own decision about this. Take your time and think it over carefully, and then write and let me know if I should come for you.

Sincerely and affectionately yours,

George Martin

P.S. I've hired Lizzy as my housekeeper.

A feeling of elation swept over Will. He could go back to Winchester! He'd see Matt almost every day, and there'd be school in the fall! He closed his eyes and pictured the high-ceilinged, well-furnished rooms of Doc's large brick house and Lizzy there to pamper him like she had in the old days at home.

But what would his aunt's family say when he told them he was leaving? He hoped they wouldn't think that he was ungrateful—or that he couldn't take the hard work. Meg would miss him most, but Aunt Ella, too, would be sorry to see him go. And Uncle Jed? He wondered if his uncle would miss his help or would simply be relieved to have one less mouth to feed this winter.

"Doc Martin said to take my time and think it over carefully," Will said aloud. "I don't have to tell them anything yet." Stuffing the letter in his pocket, he picked up his fishing pole and started toward home, seeing broad streets lined with homes and shops instead of the narrow, tree-shaded dirt road under his feet. It would be wonderful to be back in Winchester again!

He wondered if Doc Martin's sister would be as nice as Aunt Ella. Probably not, since she wasn't family. Family! Why, Aunt Ella was his closest relative now. When he went to live with Doc, he'd be leaving behind all the family he had left. Could a bachelor doctor, his widowed sister, and a boy be a family? he wondered. He knew how lonely it was to be the only young person in a house.

Suddenly Will realized how much he was going to miss Meg. She wasn't silly and helpless like other girls he'd known—or like his sisters, he thought with a pang. Was it because she was a country girl, or because she'd always been expected to do her share in a family with no slaves—a family that actually took pride in working hard?

Working hard. Will made a fist and flexed his muscles. He was proud of his body's new strength and toughness, even of the calluses the garden tools had worn on his hands. Yes, he'd learned to work hard, but not as hard as his uncle. That man could really work! And he knew how to do almost everything.

Hadn't he been the one to fix the millworks when the miller himself couldn't do it?

With a jolt, Will realized that he was proud of Uncle Jed! That during the weeks they'd worked together he'd come to respect his uncle! He hadn't meant for that to happen. How could Will Page, son of a fallen Confederate patriot, respect a man who'd refused to fight?

Before Will could sort out his feelings, he was wading across the little stream that crossed the road at the edge of his uncle's property. From the lane, he saw Aunt Ella going toward the house with a serving bowl. He was even later than he'd thought! He put the fishing pole in the barn and ran to the porch to wash. The family was already at the table when he came inside.

"I'm sorry I'm late, Aunt Ella."

"We were beginning to worry about you, Will," she said.

He passed his plate, and his uncle filled it with a large serving of squirrel stew and dumplings.

"I'm glad you had good luck hunting," Will said. "The bugs were biting down at the pond, but the fish sure weren't."

"Well, at least you got the butter," said Meg.

Will's heart sank. The butter! How could he have forgotten the butter?

"You did get the butter, didn't you?"

"Now, Meg, Will can't help it if Mrs. Brown hasn't done her churning yet," said Aunt Ella.

"I—I forgot," Will said lamely.

"You mean you left it down where you were fishing?" Meg's voice rose.

Will shook his head. "I was supposed to go back to the

house for it when I finished," he said miserably. "And I forgot to." Why, oh, why couldn't he have kept his mouth shut and let them think Mrs. Brown hadn't churned yet?

"Well, no harm's done," Aunt Ella said. "Meg can walk over tomorrow and pick it up."

"Oh, good!" Meg cried. Then, turning to Will, she said, "But I still don't see how you could just walk off and forget it."

"Leave me alone, Meg!" Will shouted. "Just you leave me alone!" His breath came in ragged gasps. There was no other sound in the suddenly quiet room.

After what seemed like a long time, Uncle Jed cleared his throat. "Did you run into some kind of trouble down there that made you forget?"

Will nodded. And then, his voice tight with rage, he told them about Hank and the letter. When he had finished, he picked up his fork and stirred it through the stew on his plate, wondering when his stomach would unknot.

Aunt Ella finally broke the silence. "That awful, awful boy!" she said. "His father should know about this."

Will smiled wanly. "I think he does." And then he repeated his conversation with Mr. Riley at the store.

"You handled the whole thing very well, lad," Uncle Jed said when he was finished. "Very well, indeed."

His words made Will feel a little better. He picked up his fork and began to eat.

"I don't know how you could pretend you didn't care when Hank kept teasing you," Meg said, pushing away her empty plate.

Will looked across the table at her. "It's something Charlie taught me when I first started school. He said if a boy snatched my cap, I shouldn't chase him and try to get it back. He'd give up his teasing if I didn't make a fuss. I figured this was the same sort of thing." Will shook his head. "But it sure did take Hank a long time to give up—and he still wouldn't let me have the letter."

"I thought only grown-ups got mail. Who was the letter from, anyway?" Meg asked.

"From Doc Martin," Will said reluctantly. He was relieved to see Aunt Ella catch Meg's eye and give an almost imperceptible shake of her head before his cousin could ask anything more.

In his room a short time later, Will reread Doc's letter. His eyes lingered on the words "You're a fine boy, Will, and I'd be proud to raise you as my son." Smiling, he folded the letter and slipped it between the pages of his Bible.

The next afternoon Meg hurried through her chores and cheerfully started off toward the Browns' house. From the stump under the oak tree, Will watched her skip down the lane. He was still embarrassed that he'd forgotten the butter, but he was glad his cousin had an excuse to get away for an hour or two.

Sweat trickled down his forehead. He mopped his face with his handkerchief and chose another pine log from the stack beside him. Splitting kindling was the only chore he'd been able to think of that could be done sitting down in the shade. He grinned when he heard the sound of a whetstone grinding against metal inside the barn. His uncle had found a cool place to work and a job he could do sitting down, too.

The monotonous scraping of the whetstone and the chirring of the locusts combined with the sultry heat made Will drowsy. He leaned back against the tree trunk and closed his eyes for a moment. Suddenly he heard Meg calling. He straightened up with a start and saw her hurrying up the lane, oblivious of the heat. How could she be back so soon? Then he noticed the long shadows and realized with chagrin that he must have fallen asleep. Uncle Jed appeared at the barn door, brushing straw from his clothes, and Will knew that he wasn't the only one who had napped away the heat of the day.

"We got another letter from the twins!" Meg called.

Aunt Ella dropped her sewing and hurried from her rocking chair on the porch. "You and Will can take that butter to the springhouse," she said breathlessly, reaching for the envelope.

Meg scowled. "Since when does it take two people to put a round of butter in the springhouse?" she grumbled as soon as she and Will were out of hearing distance. "And how come everybody around here is so—so *private* about their mail, anyway?"

Will didn't answer. He'd read Doc Martin's letter so many times he almost knew it by heart, but he didn't want to talk about it. How could he tell Meg that he was going to leave?

Will opened the springhouse door and they ducked inside the small building. The sudden coolness came as a welcome relief. But Meg was not easily distracted. "What did Doc Martin say in his letter, Will?"

"He—well, he said he'd hired Lizzy, our old slave, as his housekeeper. And that his sister is living with him now."

"He must have said more," said Meg, her eyes searching his face. "He did, didn't he?"

"Of course he said more!" Will burst out. "But the rest of it was personal. Can't you understand? Now hurry up and put the butter away."

Scowling again, Meg lifted the cloth-wrapped round of butter from her basket. Will leaned over and raised the lid of one of the storage crocks in the cold stream of spring water that flowed through the stone trough.

"Oh, I almost forgot!" Meg exclaimed, her face brightening. "I've got something for you." She pulled a folded napkin from the basket and handed it to him. He opened it to find a huge piece of cake. The miller's wife had sent him a treat! "Mrs. Brown asked me in for cake and milk, and when I said how good it was, she cut me another piece of cake. I told her I'd eat it on the way home, 'cause I wanted to save it for you."

Will was embarrassed. He'd never even thought of Meg yesterday when he was enjoying Mrs. Brown's apple pie.

"Go on and eat it, Will. It's delicious!"

Meg would be offended if he didn't eat the cake, but Will didn't think he deserved it. He hesitated a moment longer, then carefully broke the piece of cake in two. "Let's share it, Meg," he said.

They sat on the cool, stone floor and ate in companionable silence, picking every crumb from the napkin when they'd finished. Then they stooped and went through the low doorway into the oppressive heat.

Meg dashed off. "Let's go find out what Sam and Enos wrote," she called over her shoulder.

Will followed her to the house, wondering why hot weather never seemed to bother her. Inside, Aunt Ella and Uncle Jed were sitting silently at the table. In front of them lay the letter and several pieces of paper money. Even in the dim light, Will could see traces of tears on his aunt's face. He stopped and stood self-consciously in the doorway.

"What's the matter, Ma?" Meg asked, slipping onto the bench beside her mother.

But it was her father who answered. "The boys aren't coming home after the harvest like we'd planned. They sent us their earnings to help out, but they aren't coming home in the fall."

"Why not?" Meg asked.

Uncle Jed sighed. "The farmer they've been working for asked them to stay. Enos wrote that they figured the extra cash they'd send back would be more use to us than having them here over the winter."

"But I miss them so much," Meg whispered.

Will watched his aunt slip her arm around Meg. "I miss them, too," she said. "It's a good thing we have Will with us." Looking up, she said, "Come and sit here beside me, Will."

Half embarrassed, half pleased, Will walked around the table and sat down on the other side of his aunt. Her hand on his arm felt cool and comforting.

Uncle Jed sighed again and said, "I guess we'll manage without the twins as long as we've got Will. He's a good worker."

Will's heart was heavy. How could he tell them he was going back to Winchester?

ELEVEN

Will climbed the attic stairs slowly. It felt strange to be going to bed in the middle of the morning, but Aunt Ella had told him to lie down while she brewed some peppermint tea to ease his stomachache. He pushed open the door and his eyes widened in surprise when he saw Meg standing in front of his table.

"What are you doing in my room?"

At the sound of his voice, she whirled around and something white fell from between the pages of his Bible.

"How dare you read my letter!" Will's voice shook with rage.

Meg faced him defiantly. "I didn't read your old letter! You know I—"

"Get out. Just get out of here!" Will's voice rose.

Head held high, Meg brushed past him and ran down the stairs. Will crossed the room and picked up the letter. He'd have to think of a better place to keep it. Then, aware of his aunt's approaching footsteps, he stuffed it into his shirt pocket.

"You're supposed to be in bed," Aunt Ella said as she came into the room with a steaming cup.

Will took the tea and set it on the table. He hoped the herbal remedy would work quickly. He felt worse than ever now.

"Meg was upset that you accused her of reading your letter," Aunt Ella said quietly. "She didn't, you know."

"She *said* she didn't, but what was she doing in my room?"

"Cleaning," Aunt Ella said.

Cleaning? And then Will saw the broom propped against the wall and the rag that had fallen to the floor near the table. Could the letter simply have fallen out of his Bible when she lifted it to dust the table?

"I—I thought she'd come to read my letter from Doc Martin. She kept asking me what he'd said," he muttered.

"Meg can't read, Will."

Meg couldn't *read?* Will sank down onto the straight chair. "I—I didn't know that," he said in a small voice.

"You knew there'd been no school here since the beginning of the war," Aunt Ella said sharply. "I told you that the day you came!"

"Yes, but I—I thought you must have taught her! Mama taught Betsy and Eleanor to read and write, and to figure, too."

"Your mama had time to teach her daughters those things. She didn't have to spend every waking minute cooking and washing and mending and cleaning and gardening. And your mama had books." Aunt Ella's voice was hard.

Will watched his aunt leave the room and thought sadly that his coming here had made her life harder still, with even more cooking and sewing and washing and cleaning. She'd probably be relieved when she found out he was leaving. Will picked up the spoon and stirred his tea again. From the window he saw his aunt go into the toolshed and come out with a hoe. She was going to finish his morning chores! Maybe when he was back in Winchester, she'd realize that he'd done his share of work around here.

He picked up the now lukewarm tea and drank several swallows. The minty aroma seemed to fill his head. He drank some more, then went to lie down. At home when he was sick, Mama would sit with him and put cool cloths on his forehead. He found himself wondering what kind of woman Doc Martin's sister was.

―――――――――――

When Will opened his eyes, his stomachache was gone. He lay quietly, listening to the family talking in the room below.

"Is the boy still sick?" It was his uncle's voice.

"He should be feeling better by now," answered Aunt Ella. "I've made some broth for Meg to take up to him."

"I'm never going in his room again. Never." His cousin's voice sounded more hurt than angry.

"Never's a long time, miss," said Aunt Ella tartly.

Will held his breath. He didn't want to face Meg yet.

"But now is too soon," came his uncle's voice. "I'll take it up to him."

Will heard his uncle's heavy tread on the stairs and felt a moment of confusion. Should he pretend he was still asleep? A sharp knock on his partially closed door was his answer. "Come in," he called, sitting up.

Uncle Jed's height made the low-ceilinged room seem even smaller. "Ella sent you this," he said, handing Will a bowl of broth. He gestured toward the envelope in Will's shirt pocket. "Is that the letter that caused all the commotion?"

Will nodded, embarrassed that his uncle knew about his terrible mistake.

"Do you know what it says?"

Will nodded again. He knew every word of it.

"Why not destroy it? Then you'd never have to worry about

anybody reading it. Or about hurting anybody's feelings because you thought they did."

Will gulped. "I'll burn it in the kitchen fire when I take over my bowl."

"Good. You can apologize to Meg while you're there."

Resentfully, Will watched his uncle leave the room. He'd have apologized without being told to!

"Thanks for making me the broth, Aunt Ella," Will said, setting his bowl and the teacup on the table. Then he turned to his cousin. "And I'm sorry I thought you'd read my letter, Meg. I didn't know you couldn't read."

Meg's eyes narrowed. "Even if I could read, I never would have read your letter! I don't care what's in it. In fact, I wouldn't bother to listen if you tried to tell me!"

Will backed away, realizing that he had only made things worse. "I'm going to burn it," he said, walking to the hearth and laying the envelope on the still-glowing coals. He stood for a moment, watching it crumple and blacken into ash. Then he turned and saw Meg and Aunt Ella watching him. He wanted to say something, but he didn't know what.

It was Meg who broke the silence. "Now you won't ever have to worry about anybody reading your precious letter, will you?"

Aunt Ella sighed and added his dishes to her dishpan. Uncomfortable in the strained silence, Will hurried out of the kitchen and went to help his uncle with the pasture fence.

"You sure you feel like working? You don't look so good."

"I'm fine," Will said shortly.

Uncle Jed looked toward the kitchen and then back at Will. "By tomorrow it will all be forgotten, lad. 'Cept maybe by you," he added, reaching for a post.

TWELVE

"How far is it to Enos and Sam's fishing place?" Will asked as he and Meg set off for the river the next afternoon.

"'Bout as far as to the millpond, but it's mostly through the woods. We leave the road here by this dead poplar tree."

Will followed his cousin, hoping she knew where she was going. He couldn't see any sign of a path through the dense woods, or any landmarks, either. Then he spotted a tree with a notch cut in the bark. Of course! The twins had blazed the way. He wouldn't have to worry about Meg getting them lost— or about not being able to find his way to the river when he went alone.

Finally they turned onto a narrow path that led them to a stream. "The best fishing spot's just a little way from here," Meg said.

"This—this is the river?" Will asked.

"Of course it's the river! What did you expect?"

Will thought of the beautiful Shenandoah, winding its way through the Valley. "Something a little wider, I guess. At home, our *creeks* are bigger than this."

Meg faced him angrily. "Everything was bigger and better back home, wasn't it? It's too bad somebody in wonderful Winchester didn't take you in when your ma died!"

"Mama left a letter saying she wanted me to come here," Will said shortly.

"That doesn't make any sense at all! Why would she send you here after she'd been returning my ma's letters without even opening them?"

"I think it was Papa who returned those letters."

"Then I'll bet it didn't matter to her whether Pa was in the war or not!" Meg said triumphantly. "And it shouldn't matter to you, either."

Will looked away. "Maybe it shouldn't, but it does. Now, are you going to show me that fishing spot, or not?"

Meg led the way upstream along the riverbank. Will knew from the stiffness of her back how angry she was. He couldn't help wondering if she was right about Mama not caring that Uncle Jed hadn't fought for the South. He was so lost in thought that he almost bumped into Meg when she stopped abruptly.

"Well, look who's here!" said a mocking voice. There, coming toward them, were Hank and Patrick, each carrying a fish.

"Looks like you had good luck today," Will said, eyeing the fish. "Where's Amos?"

"He's sick," Patrick said. "Where's Charlie?"

"He's dead." Will's voice was steady, but his pulse pounded as if he'd been running.

Meg gasped, and Hank turned to her. " 'My ma's got a cousin named Charles,' " he mimicked, " 'but nobody calls him Charlie.' You little liar!"

"That wasn't a lie!" Meg said, moving closer to Will. "Ma does have a cousin named Charles!"

"That's twice she's lied now," said Patrick.

"Yeah," said Hank. "Don't you know what happens to little girls who tell lies?"

Will stepped forward. "Leave her alone, Hank."

"You gonna make me?"

For once, Will didn't know what to say. He had to look out for Meg, but— His heart seemed to skip a beat when Hank stooped over to pick up a small piece of bark, placed it on his shoulder, and stared at him defiantly.

Will swallowed hard. He'd been dreading something like this ever since he met Hank and his friends. But at least it wouldn't be three against one. And he'd rather lose a fight than have Hank and Patrick—and Meg—think he was a coward. Accepting Hank's challenge, he knocked the chip off his shoulder. Warily, the two boys faced each other. Then Will lunged. But Hank was quicker than he, and Will found himself sprawled flat on the ground before he could land a blow.

"You tripped me!" he said, gasping for breath as he struggled to sit up. "Don't you know how to fight fair?"

"I know how to win!" Hank said boastfully, pushing him back to the ground with his foot.

Again Will tried to get up, and again Hank pushed him down. Rolling sideways, Will scrambled to his feet and stood facing his adversary. "You know what you are, Hank?" he said through clenched teeth. "You're a poor sport and—and a coward!"

Hank sprang on him like a cat. Will crashed to the ground again, this time with Hank on top of him, pummeling his face and chest as if he would never stop. Finally, Patrick pulled Hank away.

"Geez, Hank, you don't want to kill him, do you?"

Will struggled to sit up, but Hank broke away from Patrick. Placing his bare foot on Will's chest, Hank pushed him back to the ground and stood glaring down at him. "Don't you ever call me a coward again, Will-yum Page! There ain't no cowards in *my* family."

Will waited until Hank and Patrick picked up their fish and their poles and started down the path before he tried to sit up again. His head was swimming, and he could taste the blood from a badly split lip. Someday, somehow, he'd get even with Hank!

Meg knelt beside him, weeping. "It's my fault! It's all my fault!" She tried to wipe his face with her hanky, but he pushed her away.

"It didn't have anything to do with you, Meg," he said, gingerly feeling his swollen lip.

"But—"

"Hank's been wanting to get the best of me ever since I came here. He didn't need much of an excuse to beat me up." Will hauled himself to his feet, but his head swam so that he had to lean against a tree.

"Shall I get Pa?" Meg asked in a small voice.

"I can walk," Will said. But he didn't object when Meg carried his fishing pole and the bait jar.

By the time they reached home, Will's eyes were almost swollen shut and his throbbing head felt about twice its normal size. Aunt Ella hurried to his side. "What happened? Was there an accident?"

Will started to shake his head, but decided against it. "I'm all right," he said weakly.

Aunt Ella settled him in the rocking chair on the porch and began bathing his face with cool water while Meg told what had happened. Aunt Ella turned to her husband, who had been listening intently. "Jed, this time Hank has gone too far. If you won't speak to Mr. Riley, I will."

"You wouldn't be doing Will any favor if you did. Think how those boys would torment him if his auntie complained that Hank had beaten him up. I don't like it any better than you do, Ella, but this is something Will has to handle by himself."

Turning to Will, Uncle Jed said, "From what Meg told us, Hank didn't do all this damage until you called him a coward. What did you do that for?"

Will hung his head. "I was angry at him for tripping me, and it was the worst thing I could think of to call him, in front of Meg."

Uncle Jed stood up. "Well, maybe you've learned a lesson. Nobody wants to be called a coward—or thought one—when he's not."

"Do you feel well enough to help Meg and me clear the weeds out of the graveyard this morning?" Aunt Ella asked after breakfast the next day. "Your uncle will walk the trap line for you."

Will nodded. "I look a lot worse than I feel," he said. His face was swollen and discolored by bruises in spite of the poultice Aunt Ella had made for him.

"Come on out and I'll show you how to sharpen the sickle, Will," Uncle Jed said as Meg jumped up and began clearing the table, eager for a morning away from the house.

Soon the three of them were on their way. "I didn't know you had a graveyard," Will said as they walked single file along an overgrown path that ran east from the fallow field.

102

"Beth's buried there, and Grandma and Grandpa Jones, and Pa's two brothers that died when they were young, and some cousins I never knew," Meg explained.

A small fenced clearing lay on a knoll in the woods ahead, and Will could see several grave markers rising above the tall grass. "It looks like our work's cut out for us," Aunt Ella said.

"Here's where Beth lies," said Meg, dropping to her knees beside two closely placed slabs of fieldstone. "Someday we'll have a proper memorial stone, but for now. . . . " Her voice faded away.

Will didn't know what to say, so he squatted down before the larger stone and traced the letters and numbers that had been scratched into its surface: B.J., 1859–1863.

Aunt Ella set down a basket of oval-leafed plants like the ones that covered the ground on the shady side of the house and knelt to pull the ragweed and sorrel from around her little daughter's grave. Her face was sad, but peaceful. Meg pointed out her grandparents' graves and those of the other relatives, but Will scarcely listened. He was watching Aunt Ella.

When Meg began to pull the weeds around the other graves, Will set to work cutting the grass between the stones and the split rail fence that enclosed the small graveyard. He wondered if the grass had grown up around the plain white stone where his father was buried near the Middletown Road.

He thought of the new graves in the Page family plot at the churchyard—Charlie's stone, with "Gone, But Not Forgotten" engraved across the bottom, and the two small white markers topped by carefully carved lambs above where his sisters lay. And Mama's grave, which he'd never seen. Before he'd left Winchester, Doc Martin had helped Will choose the words for his mother's marker and had promised to meet with the stone carver at the marble and granite works in town—and to see that the stone was put in place when it was ready, too.

By midmorning, the work was finished. Will, Meg, and Aunt Ella stood back and admired the results of their efforts. "I'll carry water every day till that periwinkle you planted on Beth's grave takes root," Meg promised her mother as they started back along the path. Then she turned to Will. "Did working in the graveyard make you think of your family and feel sad?" she asked.

Will thought for a moment. "It made me think about them, and about how much I miss them," he said slowly, "but it didn't exactly make me feel sad. At least, not as sad as I was at first. I—I guess I've gotten used to their being gone. 'Gone, but not forgotten,' like it says on Charlie's stone."

His aunt asked, "What about the way Charlie died, Will? Are you able to accept that yet?"

Will waited for the pounding in his temples to begin, but all he felt was a sense of emptiness. "I guess I have, Aunt Ella," he said with surprise. "It was a horrible way for him to die, but I guess I've accepted it."

"It must be terrible for you when those boys taunt you about Charlie," Aunt Ella said.

"It's terrible, all right. But it's better than being pitied like I was in Winchester, and each time they say something, it's a little easier for me to take it."

Meg sighed. "I guess I shouldn't have said what I did that day at the pond when they asked if you knew a Charlie Page."

"I'm glad you did, Meg. I wasn't ready to face up to them then."

"Well, you sure faced up to Hank yesterday! If he hadn't tripped you, you'd have bloodied his nose for sure."

If only he could have gotten in just one good punch! Will touched his swollen lip. Charlie had taught him to use his wits to avoid a fight if he could, but to strike first if a fight was inevitable. He'd failed on both counts yesterday.

Aunt Ella said, "I don't understand why you wanted to fight Hank when he's so much bigger than you are."

"I didn't want to, Aunt Ella. But I had to, anyway."

"Had to, Will?"

Will looked at his aunt in surprise. "He'd frightened Meg! And he'd challenged me, too! If I hadn't fought him, he'd have thought I was a coward."

"A person thinking you're a coward doesn't make you one, Will," Aunt Ella said quietly.

Will looked away. "Maybe not, but I'd have felt like one if I hadn't fought him. And that would be a lot worse than feeling bruised and swollen."

Aunt Ella nodded. "I see," she said slowly. "Believing as you do, I guess fighting him was your only choice."

Believing as he did? Will frowned. Would he have had another choice if he believed differently?

THIRTEEN

Will was cutting the grass around the house. He swung the scythe in wide arcs, trying to maintain the easy, rhythmic movement he remembered from watching Fred. Meg sat on the porch with her favorite of the half-grown chickens in her lap. "Someone's coming, Will," she said.

Will straightened up, flexing his fingers to rest them from their tight grip on the tool's handle. Turning, he saw a tall, dark-haired man limping up the lane.

"Hey!" the man called, waving.

Will leaned his scythe against the fence and went to meet the stranger.

"I—I need a place to spend the night," the man said. "A young fellow back at the store directed me here, but he didn't say it was so far."

Under his tan, the man's skin had a grayish tint, and his eyes were sunken in his thin face, as if he'd been ill. Will wondered why the Rileys or the Browns hadn't put him up instead of sending him several miles farther on. Then the truth hit him. "You're a Yankee, aren't you?" His mouth felt dry as he spit out the words, realizing with surprise that it had been weeks since he'd thought of the hated Yankees.

The man's jaw tightened and he nodded. "Union cavalry. I was wounded just before the war ended, and now I'm finally on my way home. It's going to storm," he said, gesturing toward the lowering clouds in the western sky, "so if I could just sleep in your barn tonight. . . . " His voice faded and he swayed a little.

Meg spoke up. "Help him over to the shade while I get some water."

The man swayed again, and Will automatically grasped his arm to steady him. He led him to the stump under the oak tree where he sat to split kindling.

Just as Meg came running back from the spring with the

water, Aunt Ella hurried over from the house. Will watched the man struggle to his feet, surprised that a Yankee would have good manners.

"Sit down, sit down!" commanded Aunt Ella.

The man sank back onto the stump. His hand shook as he reached for Meg's dipper.

"Will," Aunt Ella said quickly, "go find your uncle. And you, Meg, bring me the butter from the springhouse."

Aunt Ella disappeared into the kitchen, and his cousin hurried to get the butter. Will scowled. Imagine wasting their carefully hoarded round on a Yankee! Hands in his pockets and chin thrust out, he started toward the buckwheat field. His stomach lurched at the thought of the three biscuits that had been left over from dinner, thickly smeared with golden butter, disappearing into the Yankee's mouth.

Uncle Jed came to the edge of the field to meet him. "What's wrong?" he asked.

"There's a Yankee that wants to stay the night, and—and Aunt Ella's feeding him!"

"Even Yankees got to eat," Uncle Jed said mildly.

"You—you're not going to let him stay, are you?"

Uncle Jed ignored his question. "Seems strange a Yankee going home would end up this far from the main road."

"They said at the store he should ask to stay here. Don't you see, they figured you're the only one around who'd be willing to take in a Yankee. And if you do it, you'll lose all the respect you gained by fixing the millworks!"

Uncle Jed looked down at him quizzically. After a few moments he said, "I do what I think is right without worrying as to whether it will cause me gain or loss. A man doesn't want to have to stop and try to figure out what everybody else might think or do each time he has to make a decision."

"You're going to let him stay," Will said flatly.

"Probably will. I guess some Yankee families took in my boys on their way to Ohio."

"That's not the same thing," Will argued.

"How do you figure that?"

"Sam and Enos weren't their enemies. They'd never fought against them or stolen their stock or burned—"

"Lad," said Uncle Jed, laying a hand on Will's shoulder, "The war's over. I know how you feel, but—"

Will jerked away from his uncle's touch. "No, you don't know how I feel! You didn't lose everything you cared about because of the war!"

"I didn't lose everything, the way you did," his uncle said. "I still have Ella and Meg. And the house and land. But that war cost me a daughter and two sons. And—"

"But Sam and Enos—"

"Don't interrupt me!" Uncle Jed said sharply. "Stop brooding on your own losses long enough to think about somebody else for a change! Sam and Enos are alive and healthy, and I'm thankful for that, but they're lost to Ella and me. They'll settle in Ohio. They'll marry and raise families there instead of in Virginia."

He paused and looked at Will. "How do you think I felt when my boys left home at sixteen because those two armies hadn't left us with enough food to go around?" he asked. "How do you think I felt when I realized I'd never be able to buy seed and livestock to get this place back on its feet if those boys didn't find work and send home their earnings? And how do you think I've felt when folks I've known all my life treat me like a stranger—or maybe an outlaw—because I acted on my beliefs instead of on theirs?"

Will's face burned with shame. "I guess I never thought about any of those things."

"No, you've been so busy feeding your own feelings of hate and anger that you haven't been able to think about much else."

"I—I'm sorry, sir," Will mumbled.

His uncle's jaw tightened. "I've told you not to call me 'sir,' " he said harshly.

"I forgot," Will said, unable to meet his uncle's eyes.

"Well, see that you don't forget again." Uncle Jed turned on his heel and started toward the house.

Will followed several paces behind him. He was shaken by his uncle's anger and by the realization of how self-centered he'd been. He'd never given a thought to how Uncle Jed might feel! He wished he hadn't slipped and said "sir"—there was no need to be so obvious about not wanting to call his uncle by name.

When they reached the corner of the springhouse, Uncle Jed lengthened his stride and walked toward the stranger. The young man struggled to his feet and held out his hand. "James Woodley, from Pennsylvania," he said.

Uncle Jed shook hands with him. "Jed Jones," he said. "I understand you need a place to stay the night. From the looks of you, better plan on resting here a week or so before you go on."

Without waiting to hear more, Will turned and went back to the yard. He welcomed the thought of physical exertion, and as he watched the grass fall before the scythe he tried not to think about his confrontation with Uncle Jed. But it was hard to put his uncle's words out of his mind.

When he went inside for supper, the sight of the table set for five made Will's stomach knot up as if he had been punched. "I'm going upstairs, Aunt Ella," he said stiffly. "All of a sudden I'm not hungry anymore."

It was hot in his attic room. Hot and stuffy. Quietly he opened the door he'd slammed as he came in, hoping to create some cross ventilation, though the air outside was oppressively still. From downstairs he heard the stranger's voice. "Isn't your son eating with us?"

"Will's my nephew from Winchester. He lost his family, so he came to us."

"Winchester! No wonder he was so unhappy to see me! People there suffered terribly during the Union occupation."

Will hesitated at the door, half tempted to stand there and listen, but he heard Aunt Ella say, "Take this on up to him, Meg. He's bound to be hungry after scything the yard." Tiptoeing to the bed, Will lay down with his arm across his face. He heard his cousin's bare feet on the steep stairs and her timid knock at his open door. Sitting up, he turned toward her and blinked, hoping she'd think she'd awakened him.

"Ma sent you up a plate," she whispered. "I'll just leave it on your table so you can eat it when you're ready."

Will felt a wave of affection for his cousin. "Thanks, Meg," he said. "I guess I'm hungrier than I thought I was."

She looked at him levelly. "When you come to breakfast in the morning, I think you'll find that Jim's a good person even if he is a Yankee."

110

"So it's 'Jim' now."

Meg nodded. "He said that's what his family calls him. Since he'll be here awhile, Ma asked him."

"So now we have to stretch what little food there is to feed five, do we?"

"We have plenty of food now with the garden and the summer apples. And, anyway, you didn't seem to worry about stretching the food when you came here, Will Page!"

Will's face flushed as he remembered the few wizened potatoes that had been in the root cellar the day he'd arrived and how willing the family had been to share what little they had.

"Don't worry, Will. I know you didn't mean to sound so selfish. I know you'd gladly go hungry for a week if Jim had fought for the South and that it's having a Yankee under the same roof that's upset you."

Under the same roof! "Where— Where's this 'Jim' going to sleep?" he whispered.

"He said he'd sleep in the barn. He understands how you feel."

Will waited until the sound of Meg's footsteps on the stairs had faded away before he got up and ate his solitary meal. He wasn't so sure that he liked being understood.

That night, Will awoke during a violent storm. He climbed out of bed and hurried to close the window. A flash of lightning illuminated the yard, and for a moment the outbuildings were silhouetted against its brightness. Will thought about the Yankee soldier sleeping—or perhaps lying wakefully—in the barn.

Back in bed, he found sleep impossible. It seemed like hours before the storm faded into the distance, and then all at once it was morning and the light was streaming in his window. As soon as he opened his eyes, Will remembered the Yankee. He slipped out of bed and pulled on his clothes. How would he get through the day? Through the week? Meg had made it clear that he would be expected to eat with the Yankee—with "Jim." Picking up his supper plate and fork, he hurried down the narrow stairs and across the wet grass to the kitchen.

"Thanks for sending my supper up last night, Aunt Ella," he said, setting the dishes on the narrow table.

His aunt wiped the flour off her hands and said, "From now on, though, you'll sit at the table with the rest of us."

Will nodded, staring at the floor.

"You know, Will," Aunt Ella continued, "which side a man fought on in the war was nothing more than an accident of geography. If your father had been born in Pennsylvania or Michigan instead of in Virginia, he'd have fought just as bravely for the Union as he did for the Confederacy."

Will stared at his aunt, appalled at the thought.

She laid a hand on his arm. "There were good men fighting on both sides, Will. And some good men didn't fight at all. One of these days, I hope you'll understand that."

"None of the Yankee soldiers I ever heard about were good men," Will said, "and I saw a lot of them when they held Winchester. They were rude and cruel, and they—"

"Rude, cruel men made rude, cruel soldiers—and honorable men made honorable soldiers—no matter which army they were in," Aunt Ella said firmly. "Now, take that bucket and bring me some water."

Will started toward the spring. How dare Aunt Ella imagine his father as a Yankee soldier!

His morning chores finished, Will was washing up at the dishpan on the porch railing when Meg carried over a platter. "It's the last of the eggs Mrs. Brown sent. Ma scrambled them," she said.

Four eggs, split five ways, Will thought glumly as he went inside. The table was set with an extra plate, as he'd known it would be, but the Yankee soldier was nowhere to be seen.

"Shall I go over to the barn and get Jim?" asked Meg.

Her father shook his head. "Let Will go for him."

Sullenly, Will crossed the yard and squished through the mud to the barn. He paused at the door, wondering if he should knock, then pushed it open and stepped inside.

"Good morning," a voice said. There on a blanket-covered pile of straw sat Jim. He was reading a book in the dim light from the high window.

Will cleared his throat. "It's breakfast time," he said.

"I'll have a bite to eat in the kitchen while your aunt's cleaning up," Jim said, a finger marking his place in the book.

"They want you to eat now."

For a moment the young man hesitated. Then he noted his page number, closed the book, and struggled to his feet. Wincing as he stood, he said apologetically, "It's always worse in the morning."

Will turned and started back to the house with the Yankee limping behind him. He was relieved to find Meg sitting beside his place. At least he wouldn't have to sit next to the Yankee.

As he listened to the cheerful chorus of good mornings, Will wondered how his aunt's family could like a Yankee, after they'd lost so much to Yankee foragers. Confederate scouts had taken a lot, too, he remembered, but that was different. Will took a mouthful of the scrambled eggs. He shaved off a sliver of butter and spread it on a biscuit, noticing that Jim had slathered on so much butter that it was dripping off his biscuit in a thin, golden stream.

Jim sighed contentedly. "You don't know how long it's been since I've tasted eggs or had fresh butter on hot biscuits, ma'am."

Not much longer than it had been for the rest of them, Will thought. But he didn't dare say it.

Aunt Ella beamed. "It's been a long time since I've had a young man to appreciate my cooking."

Will looked at her in disbelief. What about him? Didn't he count?

"You must really miss your sons," Jim said sympathetically.

Aunt Ella nodded. "This house was a sad place after those boys set off. I don't think any of us really cheered up until Will arrived. Here, Will," she went on, "go ahead and finish up this last biscuit."

He took it, a little surprised that sitting at the table with a Yankee hadn't ruined his appetite.

That morning, Will helped his uncle clear the thistles from the pasture, a job he hated. The pinkish-lavender blooms were pretty, but the roots of the fast-spreading weeds went straight down, and digging them out was arduous work. After what seemed like hours, Will went to the spring to cool off. He glanced toward the house and saw Aunt Ella and Meg sitting on the porch with their mending while the Yankee lounged on the steps. The sound of their laughter followed him as he walked slowly back to the pasture.

When they all sat down to dinner at noon, Meg showed Will the tiny basket Jim had given her. "He carved it from a peach seed," she said, running her finger along its delicate handle. "And you should see the lovely things he carved from bone!"

Jim looked embarrassed. "Carving helped pass the time during the months I spent in the hospital," he said.

"Go on, show him!" Meg urged.

"I doubt that Will is interested, Meg," Jim said.

Torn between his desire to snub the Yankee and his reluctance to have Meg think him rude, Will mumbled, "Let's see what you made."

Jim reached into his pocket and pulled out a small cloth bag. Loosening the drawstring tie, he poured onto the table a dozen or so tiny carved blossoms.

Meg picked one up and turned it over so Will could see the tiny loop on the back. "They're buttons! See?"

Will was impressed in spite of himself.

"Show him the brooch, Jim," said Aunt Ella.

They all leaned forward as Jim set on the table a small oval with a raised design of a leaping doe.

"That's a fine piece of craft if I ever saw one!" Uncle Jed exclaimed.

"It's for his sweetheart," Meg said.

Blushing, Jim replaced it in the bag and began to gather up the buttons.

Uncle Jed turned to Will. "I'm not working on that fence this afternoon, so I won't be needing you," he said.

Will quickly pushed his chair back from the table. "Then I'll go fish at the river." As he started out the door he turned and said, "That rabbit pie was real good, Aunt Ella."

"Why, thank you, Will," his aunt replied, and the surprised pleasure in her voice made him realize how seldom he showed any appreciation for all she did for him. No wonder she was glad to have that polite Yankee visitor, he thought wretchedly.

Will took the fishing pole he now thought of as his own and set off. At the dead poplar tree, he turned into the woods and followed the blaze marks, thinking of his first trip to the river. It was one thing to be beaten in a fair fight, but for Hank Riley to trip him and then to push him back with his foot when he'd tried to get up—well, that was something else!

When he reached the fishing spot, Will realized that in his hurry to leave, he'd forgotten to bring bait. Glumly, he sprawled on the grassy bank, propped his elbows on the ground, and rested his chin in his hands. Less than one day of the Yankee soldier's "visit" had passed. How was he going to live through six more?

Maybe he should go back to Winchester right now, he thought as he watched the little eddies created by a partially submerged log. But even if he wrote to Doc Martin today, there was no way Doc could get the letter and come here before the Yankee's week was over. Will sighed. He'd just have to put up with him. When he did go back, though, there would be so much to tell Matt! He tried to imagine what his friend would say when he heard that Uncle Jed took in a Yankee soldier.

With a jolt, Will realized that Uncle Jed wasn't doing anything the people of Winchester hadn't done throughout the war. He remembered how his mother and the other women had fed the wounded soldiers who straggled through town for days after the battle at Sharpsburg, not caring in the least whether they were Confederate or Yankee. They were just young men in need of help.

Jim Woodley had certainly been in need of help when he arrived yesterday, Will thought, ashamed now that he'd wanted Uncle Jed to turn him away. Taking him in was the decent thing to do, he realized, and Uncle Jed was just about the most decent person he'd ever known—in spite of his refusal to fight for the South. Will figured that he had to accept the Yankee's presence, but that didn't mean he had to be friendly, the way the others were. He'd avoid the man whenever he could.

Will stared into the water. He wished Matt were there. "Maybe I could write to him," he said aloud, thinking of the blank sheets of paper at the back of his copybook. But what would he say? Matt wouldn't be interested in hearing about Meg and Aunt Ella, and Will couldn't tell him much about his uncle without sounding disloyal. It would be hard to explain about the trap line or how he was helping to repair the fence, and he certainly didn't want to write about Hank. All that was left to say was that he missed Matt a lot and wished they could go fishing and swimming together the way they used to. That wouldn't be much of a letter.

Anyway, he thought, picking up his fishing rod and starting for home, if he was going to write to anyone, it should be Doc Martin. Why did he keep putting that off?

FOURTEEN

Will finished his supper quickly that evening and excused himself, saying that he needed to split some kindling. He knew the others would linger at the table, talking, and he wanted no part of that. While he was carrying the pine logs out of the woodshed, he heard the door slam and glanced toward the house. To his surprise, he saw Jim starting down the porch steps. Will sat with his back to the barn door so that he wouldn't have to speak to Jim as he went by. It seemed a long time before he heard the creaking sound that told him the Yankee had gone inside the barn. But then the door creaked again. Glancing behind him, Will saw Jim approaching, carrying a small, three-legged milking stool.

"Thought I'd keep you company for a while," Jim said.

"I like being by myself," Will said. With satisfaction, he saw Jim's face redden and his lips tighten. Methodically, Will began to splinter off strips of pine.

At last Jim spoke. "Virginia certainly is a beautiful state."

"It was a lot more beautiful before the war. You should have seen the Shenandoah Valley before Sheridan ruined it."

Jim drew a long breath. "I did see it, Will. My unit was with Sheridan in the Valley."

Will felt the blood drain from his face. His hand tightened around the handle of the hatchet, and he jumped to his feet. His eyes, burning with hatred, met Jim's.

"Sit down, Will," Jim said quietly. "I'm going to tell you about it."

Feeling light-headed, Will stood uncertainly, looking down at the seated man. He didn't want to hear Jim's story, but there was something commanding in the Yankee's quiet voice. Will returned to his seat on the stump. "Go on, then," he said coldly.

"We were there in September of sixty-four," Jim began, "and our orders were to destroy the breadbasket of the Confederacy, to help bring an end to the war by making it impossible for Southern forces to get the food they needed to continue their fight."

Will interrupted. "To make the Valley so desolate that a crow flying across it would have to carry its own provisions," he said, paraphrasing General Sheridan's famous boast.

Jim went on as if he hadn't heard him. "We were told to drive off the livestock and destroy the crops, to burn the barns and mills—but not the houses—and to leave each farm with only enough food to last the family through the coming winter."

Will had heard all this before. He put a bored expression on his face.

"We were told to pile bales of hay around the barns and then to light them," Jim continued. "And we had to follow our orders. But the orders didn't say how close we had to pile those hay bales, or that we couldn't soak them with water before we threw a burning torch on them and went on to the next farm."

"You—you did that?" Will asked in disbelief. "*Yankees* did that?"

Jim nodded. "Whatever my unit could spare without disobeying the letter of our orders, we spared. And I know for

119

a fact that when the mill at Edinburg was torched, Union officers quartered in town helped put out the fire."

"Then how come the Valley looked like it did when I came through it two months ago?" Will challenged. "I didn't see any barns or mills, and there were plenty of houses that had been burned!" Well, some houses, anyway.

Jim sighed. "The spoiling of the Valley was one of the tragedies of the war. But you know, Will, I'm convinced that some of the destruction that was blamed on Sheridan's forces was done by bandits, especially in out-of-the-way places."

"Do you really expect me to believe that?" The corners of Will's mouth curled down in disdain. "I'm not going to listen to any more of this!"

He stalked toward the house, leaving the hatchet and the logs scattered on the ground. A few minutes later he saw from his window that Jim had moved to the stump and was chopping the kindling while Meg sat across from him on the milking stool.

Will threw himself down on the bed. When the miller's helper told him how he'd helped burn that town in Pennsylvania, he'd seemed almost proud of what he'd done. But just now Jim Woodley had seemed sorry for his part in destroying the Valley. It didn't make any sense at all!

————————

The next morning, Aunt Ella sent Meg and Will to the orchard to gather the apples that had fallen during the storm. They filled four baskets and dragged them back to the house on the slide.

After dinner Aunt Ella said, "This afternoon you children can peel and slice those windfall apples for drying."

"I'll help them," Jim said.

Will's face fell, but Meg was delighted. "Oh, good! You can tell us another one of your stories!"

They worked on the porch. Will cranked the apple parer and watched the long green strip of peel spiral off and drop, trying to ignore Jim's presence. But soon he was listening as raptly as Meg to the tale Jim told. Before he knew it, the afternoon was almost over, and Meg and Jim had cored and sliced enough apples to fill a washtub with the white crescents of fruit.

Meg sighed. "I don't see how you can make up such wonderful stories!" she said.

"I didn't make this one up, Meg. It's from a book by Charles Dickens."

"Dickens! Why, I read *David Copperfield*," Will said excitedly. "And every year Mama used to read us *A Christmas Carol*."

"I enjoyed both of those. What else have you read, Will?"

Before he could answer, Uncle Jed came up the porch steps. "You'd better bury those peelings and cores at the edge of the garden so they don't attract bees," he told Will, lifting the washtub and starting off to the springhouse.

Will frowned. "I didn't know you dried apples in the springhouse," he said.

"You don't," Meg said scornfully. "He's just storing them there overnight. Tomorrow we'll spread them out on the woodshed roof, and if it's good and hot, they'll be dry by evening."

Will started for the garden with his bucket of peelings and one of cores, glad that his uncle had interrupted when he did.

It was one thing to listen to Jim's story while he was working, and quite another to sit and talk with him.

Early the next week, Jim announced at breakfast that he felt well enough to leave for home that day. Will's relief at this news was marred by Meg's evident dismay. "Don't you think you need to rest just one more day?" she asked wistfully.

"Hush, child," Aunt Ella said. "Think of his family, looking for him to come back."

"And his sweetheart," added Will, watching the expected blush color Jim's face.

Aunt Ella and Meg hurried off to the kitchen to pack Jim a lunch, and Uncle Jed walked back to the barn with him to get his knapsack. Will saw that Jim's limp was almost gone.

When he came into the house at noon, Will noted with satisfaction that the table was set for four. And then he looked more closely. There was a book beside his plate. It looked like the one Jim had been reading that first morning in the barn.

"Did you see what Jim left for you?" Meg asked. "He said it's a good story."

"*Moby Dick*," said Will, picking up the small, leather-bound book. With a pang, he thought of his mother sitting on the horsehair sofa in the parlor with Betsy leaning on one arm and Eleanor leaning on the other as she read aloud to them each evening. He and Charlie always sprawled on the rug with the checkerboard between them, pretending not to listen. . . .

Uncle Jed's voice brought Will back to the present. "Jim was sorry you weren't here to say good-bye."

Will set the book on the table.

"It's bad manners not to wish a guest well when he leaves," Uncle Jed continued. "You know that."

Will raised his head and looked across the table at him. "I should have been here," he admitted, meeting his uncle's gaze. But how could he have watched them telling Jim good-bye without being reminded of how hard it would be for him to leave for Winchester? He wasn't ready to think about that yet!

FIFTEEN

Will awoke to the sound of rain beating on the tin roof. He shivered a little as he pulled on his clothes.

At breakfast Uncle Jed announced, "It'll be too muddy to work tomorrow, so Will and I'll walk in to the store. We need to decide what to buy with that cash the twins sent."

"We've used almost all the flour, and there's hardly any salt left," Aunt Ella said. "And we need cornmeal. But be sure to save enough to buy the children shoes for winter."

Shoes for winter! Will swallowed hard. He couldn't wait much longer to tell them he was leaving.

Uncle Jed looked out at the sheets of rain. "I think this is going to keep up all day. No use planning to do anything other than stay dry."

Aunt Ella drew her shawl closer around her and said, "Yesterday I didn't think I'd ever be cool again, but today I wouldn't mind a fire. We could cook inside, too."

"I'll bring in some wood and your soup pot," Uncle Jed said.

The usually homey room seemed dreary, and Will hoped

the fire would brighten it, as well as take off the chill.

"What are we going to do all day?" Meg asked.

Her mother said, "I'll be quite happy to sit in front of the fire in my rocking chair and do a little needlework."

"Do you play checkers?" Will asked hopefully.

Meg's face lit up. She ran to the chest near the fireplace and found a small tin box and an inch-thick wooden board with alternate squares charred black. At the table, she opened the box and poured out yellow and red kernels of corn. "Do you want to be red?" she asked.

Will nodded, and they began sorting out the kernels. He thought sadly of his father's inlaid marble board and his sets of carved ivory and ebony checkers and chessmen. How he hated to think of them being sold!

"You can go first, Meg," he said.

"We'll take turns going first," she said, making her move.

Will knew Meg would be offended if he let her win, but he didn't want to beat her too badly. He pretended not to see a jump he could have taken and was shocked when his cousin's next move set up a three-for-one trade. Too late, he realized that he faced a skilled opponent.

At least she hadn't let him win, Will thought as they set up the board again a few minutes later. He was so intent on the game that he hardly noticed his uncle building a fire in the giant fireplace or Aunt Ella wiping up the water he had tracked in. And he barely glanced up when Uncle Jed came out of the bedroom in dry clothes and sat down to watch them play. Will moved his last man onto Meg's king row, and she "crowned" it by adding a second red kernel to its square. Now they both had two kings. This game, at least, would be a tie.

But five minutes later Will was trying to figure out how his cousin had beaten him again. "You're a good player, Meg," he said grudgingly.

She grinned. "I used to watch Sam and Enos play."

Will brushed a pile of kernels into his hand and poured them carefully into the tin box. He wished his uncle hadn't seen him beaten. Beaten by a ten-year-old. Beaten by a girl!

"I could show you how to get out of that trap she had you in, lad," said Uncle Jed.

Will shook his head. "I've had enough checkers for now."

"Will you play with me, then, Pa?" asked Meg.

"Not if you're going to beat me the way you beat your cousin."

Meg giggled. "Oh, Pa, you know I never beat you!" she said.

Will went up to his room and stood at the window. Outside, everything was a watery gray blur. He glanced at his pen and copybook. He would write Doc Martin and ask him to come for him just before school started. That way he could help his uncle harvest the buckwheat and fill the woodshed before he left.

But instead of beginning the letter, Will lay down on his bed and listened to the rain lashing at the window and beating on the tin roof like bursts of musket fire. He wished he were downstairs watching the game and maybe learning some new tricks. He shouldn't have said he was tired of checkers. That made him sound like a sore loser.

He shut his eyes and thought of rainy days in the cozy parlor at home, with the gas lights burning brightly. Mama would be at her desk writing letters, and his sisters would be playing with their dolls in front of the fire while he and Charlie sat at opposite ends of the sofa, reading.

Reading! Will sat up. Slowly he walked over to the little table by the window and reached for the book the Yankee soldier had left for him two weeks before. "It's foolish not to read a book just because you don't like the person who gave it to you," he said aloud. Then, feeling almost cheerful, he clattered down the stairs.

Meg was putting away the game when Will moved a chair nearer to the window to take advantage of the pale gray light.

"Is that the book Jim gave you?" she asked.

He nodded. The stiff-backed chair creaked as he sat down and opened the book. He had read only a few pages when he became aware of the silence. He glanced up to see Meg watching him from the small three-legged stool at her mother's feet. He had never seen her sit so still before. Or look so sad.

"Is it a good book?" she asked.

He nodded again. "So far." Maybe he could teach Meg to read before he left. After all, school wouldn't start till mid-October.

Returning to the book, he found it hard to concentrate. The crackling of the fire was the only sound in the room, but still he was distracted. He looked up, and again he met Meg's eyes. This time, he thought he understood.

"Would you like me to read it aloud?" he asked.

"Oh, Will! Would you?"

He glanced at his uncle. "Do you mind?"

"Don't mind a bit."

So Will cleared his throat and began. "*Moby Dick,* by Herman Melville. Chapter One:

'*Call me Ishmael. Some years ago—never mind how long precisely—having little or no money in my purse, and nothing particular to interest me on shore, I thought I would sail about a little and see the watery part of the world. . . .*'"

SIXTEEN

The next day was clear and bright and cool. Will sniffed the air appreciatively as he and Uncle Jed set out for the store after breakfast. The small stream that crossed the road was so high they had to roll their overalls up to their knees before they waded across. The current tugged at their legs and washed the sandy gravel away from under their feet. On either side of the road, the shallow ditches were running with water, and the roadside spring had overflowed, creating a wide, shallow pond.

Several men were talking in front of the store when they arrived, and two whom Will recognized from the day they'd spent at the mill returned Uncle Jed's greetings. The third said, "Heard you had a Yankee out at your place a couple weeks ago."

Will held his breath as Uncle Jed turned toward the speaker. "That's right," he said. "He was sent to us when he stopped here at the store to ask for shelter for the night."

"Stayed more than a night, though, didn't he?" the man persisted.

Uncle Jed nodded. "He stayed until he was strong enough to go on."

"I was here when he stopped by," said one of the other men. "He didn't look so good then. Kinda grayish. That Riley boy shouldn't have sent him all that extra way to your place, the shape he was in."

Will gave a sigh of relief. They didn't seem to blame Uncle Jed for taking in a Yankee!

The men chatted a few minutes longer before Uncle Jed turned to go into the store. Inside, Mr. Riley welcomed them cheerfully, but Hank just continued sweeping the wooden floor.

"The mail stage brought you folks another letter. This one's from Pennsylvania." Mr. Riley reached into the box on the shelf behind the counter and pulled out an envelope.

Uncle Jed thanked him and slipped it into his pocket.

Pennsylvania, thought Will. It must be from Jim Woodley.

"I need salt and coffee," said his uncle. "And I'd like to look at your dress goods."

Mr. Riley scooped the salt and the coffee beans from their barrels into small cloth sacks, then led the way to the back of the store, where bolts of fabric were piled on a large table.

"Glad to see you've still got that green print," said Uncle Jed. "Ella was admiring it last fall. I'll take some of that for her, and I'll need something for Meg, too."

Mr. Riley counted off the lengths of the green print and pointed to some fabric with a tiny floral pattern. "I've got this in both pink and blue. It's right nice for a young girl."

Without thinking, Will spoke up. "Get the blue. It'll match her eyes."

Behind him, Hank snickered. " 'It'll match her eyes,' " he mimicked.

Will's face flushed and his hands clenched into fists. He stole a glance at the storekeeper and saw his jaw tighten. He watched the man cut the blue flowered cloth and fold it carefully. Then, ignoring Hank, Will followed the two men back to the counter. But Hank leaned forward and purred, "It goes so very, verrry well with her beeeautiful blue eyes!"

Blinded by anger, Will stubbed his toe on a rough place on the floor and stumbled forward, nearly falling. Behind him he heard a derisive laugh. Furious, he turned and locked eyes with Hank, who was leaning insolently on his broom with a taunting grin on his face. As Will took a step toward him, he felt a hand grasp his arm. It was Mr. Riley.

"Did he trip you with that broom?" he asked in a voice that shook with anger. "Did he?"

"I—I—"

"Speak up, boy! Did he trip you or not?" The man's face was contorted with anger.

Will glanced over at Hank, who looked back at him pleadingly, his face pale and his eyes wide with fright. He thought of how Hank had teased him with Doc Martin's letter. He remembered the day at the river when Hank had beaten him up. Here, at last, was his chance to get even! He took a deep breath, stood up straight, and looked the storekeeper right in the eye. "I wasn't hurt any," he said.

Mr. Riley released his arm. "Don't want to get him in trouble, eh? Well, he got himself in trouble this time!" Then turning to his son he said, "You go on out back. I'll get my strap and be out soon as I'm through here."

"But, Pa! He—"

"Don't you 'But, Pa!' me!" roared the storekeeper. "Just get yourself out back like I told you!"

Hank dropped the broom and walked slowly toward the back door. His shoulders drooped.

"I don't know what's got into that boy," Mr. Riley said, counting out Uncle Jed's change and putting their purchases in a cloth sack. "We need to get that school open again and keep these boys so busy studying they won't have time for making trouble!" he continued. Then he turned to Will. "Here, help yourself," he said, tipping the candy jar toward him.

"I—I shouldn't take any."

"Then I guess I'll have to give it to you," Mr. Riley said. He poured a generous number of lemon and peppermint drops onto a square of paper, folded it neatly into a small package, and handed it to Will.

"Thank you, sir," Will mumbled, stuffing it in his pocket.

Uncle Jed slung the sack over his shoulder and they started toward the mill. "Aren't you going to eat your sweets?" he asked.

Will shook his head. Then from behind the store he heard the rhythmic *thwack, thwack, thwack* of a leather strap, followed by Hank's cries for mercy. Will's feelings were a complicated mixture of satisfaction and guilt. He glanced up at his uncle and then quickly looked away.

"You should have answered Mr. Riley's question either yes or no," Uncle Jed said quietly. "What you did was dishonest even though it wasn't actually a lie. And you've made it that much harder to ever make your peace with Hank."

Will didn't answer. Once he was back in Winchester, he wouldn't have to worry about Hank. But he hated having Uncle Jed think he was dishonest.

At the mill, Mr. Brown greeted them heartily, and his helper grinned at Will. "I hear your fishing days will soon be over— they're hiring a teacher, and pretty soon you and Hank and the other fellows will be back in school," he said.

Will nodded. He'd be back in school, all right—but not with Hank and Amos and Patrick. He'd be back in school with Matt!

Aunt Ella's tired face looked young again when she unwrapped the green print fabric. And Meg pounced on the blue with a cry of delight.

"Will picked that out," her father said. "He thought it matched your eyes."

Will glanced quickly at his uncle to see if he was being mocked again, but Uncle Jed was looking fondly at Meg.

She held the cloth up to her face. "Does it, Ma? Does it really?"

"Yes, it really does." Her mother smiled. "Tomorrow I'll start working it up into a dress for you."

"I can hardly wait!" Meg said. "What else is there?" she asked. "Salt, and—oh, look!" The rich smell of the coffee beans wafted from the sack she held.

"Oh, Jed! I hardly dared hope for that!" Aunt Ella said. "Get the coffee mill, Meg. We'll have some with dinner."

They sat around the table enjoying the aroma while Meg

cranked the small wooden coffee mill. And then Will remembered the candy. He pulled the paper package from his pocket and put it on the table in front of his cousin.

"There's this, too," he said.

Meg stopped grinding to open it. "Lemon drops. And peppermint drops! Here, everybody have some!"

She passed the candy around the table. When it got to Will, he hesitated, almost tasting the pungent sweetness of the lemon candies that had always been his favorites. But then he remembered Hank's cries and the sound of Mr. Riley's strap. Filled with guilt, he passed them on. Uncle Jed was right. He *had* been dishonest!

Turning to his wife and daughter, Uncle Jed said, "Will and I heard some good news today. There's talk about hiring a teacher and opening that school in the fall. Both the storekeeper and the miller's helper mentioned it."

"That's wonderful!" exclaimed Aunt Ella. "And with the twins sending us their earnings, we'll be able to pay our share! Now Will can continue his education and Meg can learn to read."

Meg burst out, "But I'll be in the same class with Patrick's little sister, Kate! And with the Nicholson boys! They're practically babies, and I'm ten years old!"

"Don't worry, Meg. School won't start till after harvest time, and I can teach you to read by then," Will said. "That way, you won't be in the beginners' class."

"Oh, thank you, Will! Can we start today?"

Will hesitated, flattered by her eagerness, then shook his head. "I'll need time to plan the lesson, don't forget."

Meg looked impressed. Then she sighed happily. "What a lot of surprises in one day!"

"I almost forgot," said Uncle Jed. He reached into his pocket and drew out an envelope.

"Another letter!" cried Meg. "That's four this summer, counting the one Will got! Who do you think it's from?"

"Only person I know in Pennsylvania is Jim Woodley." Uncle Jed slit the envelope, and as he pulled out the folded sheet of paper, something fell onto the table.

Aunt Ella caught her breath. "Why, I never saw that much money at one time before," she said.

There were a few moments of silence while they all stared at the bills. Then Uncle Jed cleared his throat and began to read:

"Dear Friends in Virginia,

I arrived home safely, having met on my second day out a stage driver who was willing to let me ride beside him across the mountains to Luray and to arrange transport from there to Martinsburg, where I borrowed money for train fare from the pastor of the Lutheran Church. Now, thanks in great part to your kindness in caring for me when I was ill, I am reunited with my family. (They had not received the letters I wrote from the hospital and were astonished to see me, having thought I'd been killed.)

Please accept the enclosed bills as one Yankee's small penance for the destruction and despoiling of so much of your beautiful state. While I understand that no amount of money could ever make up for what your family suffered as a result of the war, perhaps it can buy replacements for the milk cow and farm horse that were taken by the Union foragers.

Again, thank you for your hospitality, and God bless you all.

Yours,

Jim Woodley"

Uncle Jed refolded the letter and slipped it back into the envelope.

At last Meg broke the silence. "It was rebel scouts, not the Yankees, that got Bessie and Nell. Does that mean we have to send the money back?"

"I think Jim would be very unhappy if we sent it back for any reason," Aunt Ella said firmly.

Still Uncle Jed did not speak. He slipped the bills inside the envelope, put it on the mantel, and went outside. The others crowded around the window and watched him cross the yard. Their eyes followed him to the edge of the pasture, where he stopped and rested his folded arms on the top rail of the newly repaired fence and stood looking toward the mountains.

Aunt Ella was the first to turn away from the window. "Meg," she said briskly, "go pick some turnip greens while I start a pan of corn bread for dinner."

Meg looked at her cousin. "I told you Jim Woodley was a nice person," she said triumphantly.

"Jim Woodley is a *rich* person," Will retorted.

Meg's face flushed with anger and her eyes narrowed. "Too bad you aren't either one, Will Page!" she said. Then, turning on her heel, she started off to the garden. Will stared after her. The words seemed to echo in the quiet of the empty house. He ran outside, stumbling across the yard. He needed to find a place to be alone. The late August sun beat down on him, and he turned toward the coolest place he knew.

Inside the springhouse, he sank onto the stone floor. The last time he'd sat in this cool dimness he'd been with Meg. Meg. Now *she* was a nice person. Kind. And generous. Loyal, too. He thought of how she'd come to his rescue the time Hank had asked him if he'd known a Charlie Page in Winchester, and how she'd understood why he hadn't wanted people to know that Charlie was his brother. And then he remembered how proud of him Meg had been when he didn't show that he was afraid of the three older boys. And when he hadn't let Hank get the best of him the day he'd teased him with the letter, too. What would she think if she knew he'd tricked Hank's father into giving him a beating for something he hadn't done? She'd know for sure he wasn't very nice!

And then he thought of how Uncle Jed had reproached him, had said he was dishonest! Will leaned back against the springhouse wall and shut his eyes. Uncle Jed would never have tried to get even with Hank in such a cowardly way.

Will's eyes flew open as Meg ducked inside the springhouse. "How did you know I was here?" he asked in surprise.

"I sometimes come here to be alone, too," she said, dropping down onto the cool floor beside him. "You know I didn't mean that, Will. I only said it because I was so angry."

"What you said was true, Meg."

She shook her head. "You *are* nice, Will. You're the nicest boy I know!"

135

Compared to Hank and Amos and Patrick, maybe he was, Will thought ruefully. Taking a deep breath and letting it out with a rush, he said, "Well, I'm sure not rich!"

Meg laughed and stood up. "Come on. Dinner's ready."

Forgiving, too, Will thought as he followed his cousin back to the house. Kind, generous, loyal, and forgiving.

"Mmm," said Meg, inhaling the aroma of freshly ground coffee and passing her plate for a wedge of hot corn bread. "This meal seems almost like a celebration!"

Aunt Ella smiled and agreed, but Uncle Jed seemed strangely withdrawn. Will wondered if he'd decided what to do about Jim Woodley's money. Torn between dismay at the idea of accepting Yankee charity and awareness of how much better the family's life would be if Aunt Ella had a milk cow and Uncle Jed had a horse to help with the heavy farm work, Will was glad he didn't have to make the decision.

"Do you know yet if you're going to keep the money?" Meg asked, voicing Will's thoughts.

Uncle Jed shook his head. "I'm still thinking it over," he said. "I don't want to do something I might regret later."

Will looked down at his plate. Like what he'd done at the store this morning.

"You see, Meg," Uncle Jed went on, "If I bought the livestock and then decided I'd done the wrong thing, it would be too late to send the money back. And if I sent it back right away and then thought maybe I should have kept it, it would be too late to change my mind. I won't have any second chance if I make a mistake on this." He turned to Will. "Sometimes, though, if we admit we made a mistake, we do get a second chance."

Meg and Aunt Ella looked from Will to Uncle Jed and then exchanged a questioning glance.

Will stared down at his half-empty plate. Admit he made a mistake? Who was he supposed to admit it to, his uncle? Hank? He almost choked. He had too much pride to do that! And then he remembered what Hank had said the day he'd showed him Papa's saber and the uniform buttons: "Pride's pretty important to you, ain't it?" It was his pride—pride in his hatred of Yankees—that had changed him from "Will" back into "Will-yum Page"!

Will looked up again and met his uncle's eyes. "I—I have to go back to the store," he said. "There's something I've got to do."

He was out the door before anyone could question him. He started down the lane, muttering to himself, "I know I have to go back, but what am I going to do when I get there?" He turned onto the road and crossed the flood-swollen stream. He'd swallow his pride and admit he was wrong, but what then?

All too soon, he splashed through the flow from the roadside spring. All too soon, the mill came into view, and the boarded-up school building, and then the store. Will's steps began to falter, but he squared his shoulders and walked determinedly toward the store. He crossed its wide porch, nodding politely to the two elderly men who were chatting there, and went inside, letting the door slam behind him.

Mr. Riley looked up from behind the counter, and Hank,

who was using a feather duster on one of the high shelves, turned to stare at him with hate-filled eyes. Will's mouth felt dry.

"Well, what is it, boy?" asked Mr. Riley. "Did your uncle forget something this morning?"

Will took a deep breath. "No, sir. I—I came back to tell you that Hank didn't trip me with his broom this morning. I—"

"See, Pa? I *told* you I didn't do nothing!" Hank stumbled down from his stepstool and reached Will in three steps. "I got the worst beating I ever had 'cause you said I tripped you, and—"

"I didn't say you tripped me!" Will broke in.

Hank stared at him, speechless.

"I just didn't say you *hadn't* tripped me."

The two boys faced each other, their bodies tense. Mr. Riley cleared his throat. "Well, now," he said, "let's let bygones be bygones. Will, you can apologize, and Hank, you can accept his apology, and—"

Hank gave a harsh laugh. "Is saying he's sorry I got a beating supposed to make everything fine and dandy?"

"I'm not sorry you got a beating! I'm sorry I wasn't honest, but I'm glad you got a beating. Real glad."

"If you'd ever had a beating like my pa gives, you wouldn't—" Slowly, a grin spread across Hank's face. "Hey," he said, "you just admitted you weren't honest. I think Pa should give you a beating for that!"

Will swallowed hard, remembering the thwacking sound of Mr. Riley's belt. Then he gave a quick nod and said, "That's fair enough. I can't take away your beating, but if your pa gives me one, too, then we'll be even. Right?"

"Ri-i-i-ght," said Hank, rubbing his hands together. "And I get to watch!"

But Mr. Riley said, "Now wait a minute! I'm not laying a hand on this boy!"

"But, Pa! He just said—"

Mr. Riley shook his head adamantly. "I don't care what he said! Nobody but his uncle has the right to lay a hand on him."

Hank turned from his father to Will. "Then we'll go out to your uncle's place and let him do it."

Will gave a quick nod of agreement and they left the store together. As they walked along in awkward silence, Will wondered how his uncle would react. He didn't know which would be worse—if he refused to go along with their plan or if he agreed to it.

"I heard you had a Yankee out at your place a while back."

Will nodded.

"And your uncle let him stay a week, didn't he?"

"Well, he wasn't in any shape to go on," Will said defensively.

Hank picked up a pebble and skipped it across a large puddle in the road. "Tell me, what was it like sleepin' under the same roof as a Yankee that might of been the one that killed your pa?"

"This Yankee wasn't even in Virginia when my father was killed," Will said, remembering how relieved he'd been to learn that Jim Woodley hadn't signed up until '63. "And, anyway, he slept in the barn."

"I'm surprised your uncle didn't give him his own bed and have him sitting right there at the table with you," Hank said.

"You know my uncle wasn't for the Union, Hank Riley. He was against the war. And he took this Yankee in because he knew Yankee families had taken in Sam and Enos on their way to Ohio. And because your brother Tom had sent him all that way when he was barely able to walk! Or was it you that sent him?"

"Well, I just wondered what it was like, havin' a Yankee for a guest," said Hank, evading Will's question. "You don't have to get all het up about it."

It had been awful, Will thought, remembering. Then he said aloud, "He did sit at the table with us, and it was awful." He stooped to pick up a rock and with a flick of his wrist tossed it into a puddle at the edge of the road.

Hank picked up a rock and spit on it. "See that beech tree?"

"Which one?

"The big one just off the road on the right."

Will's eyes searched for it. "That one way down there?" he asked, pointing.

"Watch this," Hank said. He took a few running steps and let the rock fly. It hit smack in the center of the trunk and bounced back. "Bet you can't do that," he challenged.

Will's answer was to pick up a rock of his own. Calculating the distance, he hurled it at his target. It missed by inches.

"Knew you couldn't hit it!"

At least it hadn't fallen short, Will thought, stooping for another rock. "Let's try for best two out of three," he said.

But Hank's next two tries hit the tree and his own missed it narrowly. Will wished he'd left well enough alone.

"I've always been the champion rock thrower in these

parts," Hank said smugly. "Ain't nobody 'round here that can beat me."

He threw another rock down the road ahead of them, and Will followed suit. They walked on, scooping up rocks and skimming them along just above the road or making wide arcs above it.

Suddenly Hank stopped. "What's that noise?" he asked.

Will listened. "The creek. It's high after all that rain."

"I'll race you there!" Hank said, starting off.

Will pounded down the road just behind Hank. If only he could beat him! But the distance between them widened, and he realized that he was no match for the long-legged older boy.

"Are you the champion runner, too?" Will said, panting, when he reached the creek.

"Sometimes me and Pat tie," Hank said. "You could beat Amos easy, though."

"I should hope so!" Will said, thinking of the fat boy.

Hank turned back to the raging creek. "Look at this," he said, tossing in a stick and watching it swirl downstream.

Will bent over to roll up his overalls. "Come on. Have you forgotten why we're here?"

A grin spread across Hank's face and he, too, began to roll up his pant legs.

They crossed the creek and turned up the lane toward the house. Will had to make a conscious effort not to let his steps lag when he saw his uncle walking toward the toolshed.

Uncle Jed stopped when he saw them. "What can I do for you boys this afternoon?" he asked.

Will looked at Hank. "You tell him."

"Um, you see, um, back at the store this morning, Will, here, he got me a beating I didn't deserve."

"You don't think you deserved a beating?" Uncle Jed asked. Will gave him a quick look.

"I never tripped him with that broom! Honest! You can ask him yourself!" Hank said, darting a glance at Will. "Anyway, what we thought was, since I got a beating I didn't deserve, you should give Will a beating."

"Let me get this straight," said Uncle Jed. "Since you got a beating you say you didn't deserve, Will should get a beating he doesn't deserve. Is that right?"

Hank was looking at his feet again. "I, uh, I guess that's right. It would make things even, don't you see?"

Uncle Jed looked at Will. "Is this what you want, too?" Will nodded.

"Come along to the barn, then, and I'll find me a strap." The boys followed him to the barn. Will's hands were damp with sweat. He'd had his knuckles rapped with a ruler now and then at school, but he'd never had a beating. He swallowed hard and vowed silently that he wouldn't cry out the way Hank had. Or the way Charlie had the time Papa'd taken a strap to him for making off with the door to a neighbor's privy. Even now, the memory of Charlie's prank almost made Will grin.

Uncle Jed chose one of the leather straps that hung from a hook on the barn wall. Will wondered how many times his uncle would hit him. How many times had Hank's father hit him? A good many, probably, judging from how angry the man had been.

Uncle Jed turned toward him, and Will tried not to look at the strap in his hand. His mouth felt dry.

"All right, Will. Drop your overalls and hang onto the edge of that there stall. And you, Hank. Stand over by the door where you have a good view. How many whacks do you want me to give him?" he asked. "Ten or twelve? Fifteen?"

Will gripped the edge of the stall. Ten or twelve? Fifteen? Could he stand fifteen whacks without crying out?

"Aw, ferget it."

Will couldn't believe his ears.

"What do you mean, 'ferget it'?" said Uncle Jed. "I thought you wanted to see him get a beating."

"I changed my mind! Can't a feller change his mind?"

"You sure, boy?"

"Yes! Yes, I'm sure!"

Uncle Jed took a deep breath. "Well, then, Will," he said, "you'd better pull up those overalls."

Still hardly believing what he'd just heard, Will pulled them up and stuffed in his shirttail. When he turned around, Uncle Jed was hanging the strap on the hook, and Hank was already halfway down the lane.

"Hey, Hank!" he called, breaking into a run. "Wait up!"

Hank didn't wait, but Will thought he walked a little slower. When he caught up, Will said, "Say, I was wondering if you'd help me learn to throw as well as you do."

Hank snorted. "Nobody can throw as well as I do!" he said. "But I guess I can show you how I do it," he added grudgingly.

"Thanks," said Will. "Thanks a lot, Hank. I'll come by the store one day soon." He turned and started back up the lane, whistling cheerfully. Now he wouldn't feel as if he were running away from trouble when he went back to Winchester in October.

Meg came running toward him. "What did Hank want? Why'd he come back with you?" she asked breathlessly. "And what were the two of you and Pa doing in the barn?"

"It—it was just something we had to settle," Will said uncomfortably.

Meg thought a minute. Then she asked quietly, "Was it something about Pa and the war?"

Will shook his head. He wished Meg didn't ask so many questions.

"Are you sure?" she persisted.

"Well, Hank did try to make something out of your pa putting up that Yankee soldier," Will said, remembering. "But I set him straight about that."

"Set him straight? What do you mean?"

"I told him your pa had been against the war, not for the Union."

"Well! And when did you finally figure that out?"

Her question made Will stop short. When *had* he realized why Uncle Jed had refused to fight? "At first I thought your pa was for the Union," he admitted, remembering with shame how he'd regarded his uncle as a traitor.

"And then you thought he was a coward!" Meg's voice was hard.

"I—I didn't think that very long," he protested.

"Well, you had no right to think it at all!"

Will didn't know what to say. "I'm sorry, Meg," he muttered. "I guess I just didn't understand at first."

"And you understand now?"

Will nodded.

"Tell me, then," Meg demanded.

Will took a deep breath. "I understand that your pa didn't fight in the war because he thought the war was wrong."

"And what else?" Meg persisted.

"What else?" Will echoed dumbly.

Meg made an impatient gesture. "Don't you understand that it took a lot of courage for Pa *not* to go to war when all the other men did?"

Slowly, he nodded, realizing that what she said was true.

"Say it, then!"

Will took a deep breath and said, "I understand that it took a lot of courage for your pa not to go to war."

Meg nodded with satisfaction. "Ma said you'd come to your senses by and by."

Will pulled out his handkerchief and mopped his face while he watched her run back to the house. Uncle Jed came out of the barn and said, "You look like you've got a bellyache."

Will smiled ruefully. "That's probably 'cause I've had to swallow my pride so many times today."

SEVENTEEN

"Are you ready?" Meg demanded, running to meet Will as he crossed the pasture on his way back from checking the trap line.

He nodded, reaching into his pocket. "Here, I wrote out the alphabet for you, capital letters on one side and small ones on the other." He handed her a square he'd cut from the brown paper Mr. Riley had wrapped the dress goods in the day before. "The first thing you have to do is learn the alphabet."

She looked at the paper, frowned, and turned it over. "I've seen some of these," she said, indicating the capitals. "I'll show you which ones."

Will watched while she slowly ran her finger along under his carefully printed letters, pointing in turn to B, C, D, E, H, I, K, L, M, O, and Y.

"I saw them on your books," she explained.

Of course! Will thought. *HOLY BIBLE* and *MOBY DICK*. Deciding to put aside his carefully planned lesson on the alphabet, he said, "Come on inside. I'll get the books and my slate from upstairs and we'll work at the table."

A moment later, he set the Bible in front of his cousin and pointed to the gold letters on the cover. "What does this say?" he asked.

" 'Family Bible,' " she answered.

" '*Holy* Bible,' " he corrected, pointing to each word as he said it. "And what about this one?"

"That's *Moby Dick*," she answered without hesitation. Pointing to each word in turn, she said again, "*Moby Dick*. Can you read it to us again tonight?"

Will nodded. Then, pointing at the first letter he said, "This is *M*. It says 'Mmm,' like in—"

"Like in *Meg*!"

"Right," said Will. "Like in 'Meg' and 'Ma' and 'me' and—"

"Oh, Will, can you teach me to write my name?" Meg pleaded.

Will frowned. How was he going to teach Meg to read if she insisted on skipping from one thing to another like this? Maybe he should have followed his original plan.

"Please, Will?" Her eyes shone with eagerness.

Will thought of the row of little boys endlessly droning their ABC's in front of the stern pastor who had taught their classes back in Winchester. He didn't want Meg to lose her enthusiasm. "All right. I'll teach you to write your name, and mine, and your ma's and pa's, and you can learn the letters and their sounds at the same time."

He wrote her name in large, clear letters. "M—E—G, Meg. You can practice this now," he said, handing her the slate. "While we're working in the garden later on, I'll help you learn to say the alphabet. Once you know it perfectly, you can study the paper I wrote for you and learn how each letter looks."

"I'll study every evening, Will," Meg promised, clutching the slate tightly. "You'll be surprised how fast I learn to read."

"Well, we have more than five weeks till school starts," said Will, trying not to think of all the things he wanted to do before he left for Winchester.

At noon Will watched the butter melt and soak into his third piece of corn bread while he forked up the last of his turnip greens. He was the only one still eating.

Uncle Jed leaned back in his chair and announced, "Well, I've decided to keep the money Jim Woodley sent. The way I figure it, we did what we could for him when he needed help, and now he's doing what he can to help us. I don't look on keeping that money as accepting charity," he said, glancing around the table. "I look on it as accepting a gift made in friendship."

"I think you're doing the right thing, Uncle Jed."

Three pairs of eyes stared at Will in stunned silence. Then Meg turned to her father and said in a hushed voice, "Did you hear that, Pa? He called you *Uncle Jed!*"

Will turned beet red. He hadn't realized Aunt Ella and Meg had noticed that he never called his uncle by name. "Well, he *is* my uncle, isn't he? What else would I call him?" he asked crossly, trying to cover up his embarrassment.

"I'll bet you called me plenty of names inside your own head over the past couple months," said Uncle Jed.

Will took a deep breath. "I was wrong," he said. "I was wrong, and I'm sorry."

Before Will knew what was happening, Aunt Ella was hugging him. And Meg was smiling through her tears. Uncle Jed pushed back his chair. "I'm going out to the barn," he said. "Come on out when you get a chance, son."

Had Uncle Jed meant to call him "son"? Will wondered as he crossed the yard. He knew Doc Martin had meant it when he wrote, "I'd be proud to raise you as my son," because with a letter, you could work on it till it said exactly what you meant.

Inside the barn Uncle Jed looked up from cleaning a bridle. "Thought I'd better see how this leather's holding up if we're going to get a horse," he said. "I'll find out when the next livestock auction is, and we'll go in to the county seat to pick us out that horse and cow."

They checked over the wagon and the harness and then left the barn together. "Well, once we put some bedding into those